Battle of Hearts

Battle of Hearts

A Legacy of the Maguires Romance

Stella Holt

TULE
PUBLISHING

Dedication

Thank you to Meghan and Nikki
for putting up with me.

Chapter One

THE FIVE WORST words to receive via text from your boss on a Friday evening right as your shift started were *Meet me in my office.* The message was simple but carried a lot of weight.

Rory Maguire fired back the only appropriate response. *Copy. On my way.*

Exiting his SUV, Rory made his way to his captain's office in the District 7 D.C. Metro Police Headquarters building. Their district encompassed the western border of Washington, D.C. along the Potomac River. It included several prestigious neighborhoods, federal buildings, and a large, unexpected land preserve in the nation's capital. District 7 also included some of the roughest neighborhoods in D.C. and a large university campus, keeping him and his SWAT team busy. Spending the start of his shift in the captain's office wasn't ideal on several levels. He needed time to prepare as the sergeant of a fifteen-man shift. He needed to read over the activity from the previous shift and get his mind ready, an increasingly difficult task.

Walking through the heavy double doors into the alarmed foyer of headquarters, he braced for the onslaught. There was a reason officers referred to the boss's wing of headquarters as the Lion's Den. You weren't always met with a warm welcome and often felt like you might get eaten alive.

"Maguire, how's your pops doing?" The desk sergeant that controlled all access to the three main hallways where the District 7 Metro Police management sat called down to him from his elevated perch.

The raised desk gave the officer the advantage of seeing anyone before they were on top of him, a holdover from a time before they had bulletproof windows and alarmed access doors.

"He's thoroughly enjoying retirement and a very long list of to-dos my mom keeps populated for him."

The desk sergeant's face barely creased in a smile, and he nodded as if retirement were like a disease. Some police officers were just lifers and had a hard time considering there could be something after their careers were over. But sooner or later, age caught up to everyone, and mandatory retirement would get them all if they were lucky enough to survive the job.

The sergeant buzzed him through the heavy door, and he clutched the metal handle before it could re-alarm.

"The captain's waiting for you in her office."

"Thanks," he called over his shoulder.

Not wanting to get waylaid by anyone, he picked up his pace. At the end of the hallway, he knocked on the dark wooden door with the nameplate that read *Captain Sullivan*.

"Enter," she called out from behind her door.

When he popped open the door, he found his superior officer of the last five years with her eyes squinting at the two large screens on her desk.

"You wanted to see me?" he said, closing the door behind him.

Looking up, she smiled. "Rory, have a seat." She rifled through the folders on her desk and then handed him a crisp, white envelope. "I know your shift is just starting, so we'll make this brief."

"What's this?" He opened the plain envelope.

Inside, he found a commendation for valor, signed by the chief of police. Shaking his head, he met his captain's eyes.

"You could have just slipped this in my mailbox. What do you really want to see me about?" The certificate, while nice for his employee file, was pretty typical for officers on the SWAT team who tended to see a lot of action. Not to mention the leader of the most active shift. So he wasn't terribly surprised to receive an award.

She smiled, and her chair creaked as she leaned back.

"We have an opening out at training. Course director for all recruits," she said.

"Okay?"

"And I wondered if it was time for you to consider your next step. You'll be up for lieutenant in a few years, and you've done SWAT for almost a decade. I think it's time for you to broaden your breadth of experience, if you plan to climb the management ladder. Training is an essential part of leadership."

Rory shook his head. "I haven't given my next move much thought, but I never considered going out to training. Working Monday through Friday, every weekend and holiday off? It sounds more like retirement."

He couldn't help but wonder what his dad would think. A man who'd been his idol and never worked at training. His father spent years on the street and then moved up the ranks to commissioner in his thirty-year career.

"You talk to my dad about this?"

She smiled a genuine grin that made her look much younger.

"As much as I respect your father and everything he taught me, he hasn't been the commissioner for years and doesn't get to tell me how to manage my officers' careers. That said, I believe you're a born leader with the patience and humility I need at the training center. Someone I can count on."

He was surprised by his captain's brutal honesty, and yet training seemed like an easy out he didn't deserve. If he were being honest, he had been wondering about what to do next.

"Police work is a different beast since your father was on the job. Criminals have meth labs in basements of million-dollar homes, and armor-piercing ammo. There are sex traffickers, and every other night, someone wants to jump off a bridge or a building. Officers are at risk of burning out forty percent faster than ever before, and that's if they don't get shot."

"Well, when you put it like that..." He scoffed and sat back. "No offense, Captain, but are you telling me I'm washed up?"

"On the contrary, I'm telling you I need an officer with your experience and dedication to the job to train the next generation. The course needs to be updated. We need advanced tactics on de-escalation and use of force when a patrol cop is faced with these seasoned, hardened criminals. Gone are the days of writing double-parking tickets and helping Granny cross the street." She stood and moved to sit on the edge of her desk, closer to him.

"I'll think about it."

"At least consider it. A formal vacancy won't be advertised for another week. I'm looking for a five-year commitment. I need someone to sink their teeth into this and make a real effort to update our training. We've had nine officers shot this year already."

"I'll let you know what I decide." He had no choice but to at least pretend to consider the offer. It sounded like a vacation in comparison to the things he saw on the team. If he were being honest with himself, he'd been ready to leave the team for over a year but at the same time, couldn't fathom leaving his teammates behind. He didn't want to let anyone down again.

"Alright, great. Then there is just one more thing."

Rory stood and narrowed his eyes at his captain.

"You know that saying, good things come in threes?" she said with a smirk and handed him a piece of paper with an address and the name Ainsley Nash. "We just received a protection assignment. I'd prefer you do this one yourself. Ms. Nash's father is well connected, and the request came down from the commissioner. She's some media figure. I'm trying to get more details on the actual threat, but I need you to respond to that address ASAP."

Heaving a sigh, he accepted the paper. "Yes, ma'am. Any other bombs you'd like to drop on me for my Friday night?"

"That's it for now." She smiled and then turned back to

her computers.

He made a fast exit from the Lion's Den and walked twenty feet to the smaller brick building that housed the SWAT unit. His shift had just taken a turn.

Using his badge to enter the main doors, he was greeted by the team's memorial hallway. Pictures of teammates that had fallen, awards, and a large American flag hung along the wall before he entered the large locker room. Usually, at the beginning of every shift, he unlocked his rifle from one of the huge metal gun safes and placed his tactical bulletproof vest on. The vest held his radio, several magazines filled with additional ammo, and two steel plates that were designed to withstand a lethal gunshot. The routine was literally like putting on a forty-pound weight, and his back muscles instantly tensed. But now that he was pulling a protection assignment, he could forgo his full gear. They were expected to maintain a lower profile on protection. For now, he only had his thigh rig, which held his pistol, and a few smaller magazines on his belt next to his badge.

"I saw you head into the Lion's Den. What did the captain want?" Jake, his fellow teammate of eight years, asked from a table where he sat cleaning an M4 rifle that lay in pieces on a pristine white cloth.

"To ruin my night with a protection assignment for some socialite."

"Who is the mark?" Jake asked, his eyes never leaving the task at hand.

"A senator's daughter, Nash something," Rory said as he started to pace. For some reason, this assignment was annoying him more than normal. He didn't like surprises.

He just wanted to prep his team for what would no doubt be a busy Friday night in a city with one of the highest crime rates in the nation, not feed some senator's ego.

"Senator Nash, Head of the Ethics Committee, the millionaire turned politician from upstate New York? That Senator Nash?"

Rory stopped in his tracks and faced Jake, who was steadfast in the methodical inspection of his weapon before he put the pieces back together with swift expertise.

"Damn it, the Capitol Police should be handling this. They cover the politicians and we protect the citizens of D.C.," Rory grumbled.

"You may wanna do a little online recon on which of the Nash daughters we're being assigned to, but I'll gladly volunteer for either." Jake moved to the safe to put away the firearm.

"You follow politics too closely if you know what every senator's family looks like."

"Senator Nash has been named as a possible presidential candidate. Pictures of him and his family have been all over the news."

"I prefer a newspaper," Rory said, earning a laugh from Jake.

Stomping back to his desk, he typed in the senator's name. Dozens of family pictures popped up of the tall and poised Senator Nash, surrounded by three beautiful women. All three women had dark, almost-black hair, curves, and smiled back at the camera like they knew it was going to capture their beauty.

"Damn it."

Jake walked around the desk to view the photos as Rory scrolled.

"I'm sure any of the men would be happy to accept this assignment." Jake laughed.

Looking at the sheet of paper with the address on it, he compared it to the website that popped up for a local D.C. news station.

"It gets worse." He typed in the senator's daughter's name, Ainsley Nash. His screen was covered in professional media shots from the local news network. "She's a news anchor for the D.C. metro news."

Jake looked over his shoulder at the media site as he read the information listed below her headshot aloud. "Research journalist and anchor for the morning news, Ms. Nash covers hard-hitting truth in a political town mired in scandal."

"Pretty bold for a senator's daughter to be a reporter and claim to oust corruption," Jake said.

"This just means she'll be a high-profile pain in the ass, which is why the captain said it had to be me."

"She could smear this department all over this town. One misstep, and you'll be the morning news," Jake said. "On the other hand, maybe you could use that Maguire charm to win her over and get some good press for the police department." Jake punched his arm.

"Charm?" he said.

Jake turned back. "On second thought, why don't you just lie low, figure out which of her boyfriends are bothering her, and keep your mouth shut? You're not exactly known for being suave."

"I don't need to charm anyone, and I'll play this by the book just like any other assignment." Rory packed up his laptop and gathered his things.

"You're going now?" Jake said.

"Captain said I needed to respond to Ms. Nash's office and not let her out of my sight until I hear back from the brass. The family has connections in the commissioner's office."

Jake laughed. "You're so screwed but don't worry about the team, I'll manage without you tonight. Just try not to get yourself fired this week. We need you in the First Responder Bowl next month."

"This won't take that long. If there is a real threat, the feds will want all the glory, and if there isn't, Senator Nash can hire a private babysitter."

"Just make sure you don't fall for the baby," Jake called after him.

Rory could hear Jake's laughter down the hall. Protection details were the worst assignments. As a sergeant of the D.C. Metro Emergency Response Team, he dealt with every kind of emergency: death threats, bombs, jumpers, hostage situations, and school shootings. Playing glorified bodyguard wasn't police work.

Annoyed with the turn of events for his Friday night shift, Rory gunned his supercharged, blacked-out SUV. The last thing he needed was to kowtow to some elitist gorgeous woman who didn't have a clue what a real threat was.

Chapter Two

L ETTING OUT A deep breath, Ainsley double-checked her
side mirrors, then the rearview mirror before unlocking
her car door. The parking garage was dimly lit, but there was
no one in sight. Her pulsing heart was finally finding a
normal cadence, and her adrenaline crashed. Meeting with a
source was always a rush, but this particular source came
with a real dose of intrigue because they were the key to her
latest corruption story. A series that was sending D.C.
politicians into a frenzy, and she hoped would get her
noticed by the network.

She always craved the thrill of discovering a story with
real teeth, but this one was the biggest of her career so far.
Exposing government contracts that were given to specific
companies without due process was big enough, but if she
could figure out which politicians were writing bills in an
effort to directly influence the market for their own gain, it
could be her golden ticket to a prime-time slot.

As long as she could prove it.

Developing sources was crucial, but validating the money
trail was essential. As much as she hated to admit it, her
unique access to the political circles via her family name was
how she uncovered this story in the first place. The amount

of gossip a person could learn in the ladies' room at social elite events or charity balls would astound most people. One disgruntled aid and two martinis had earned Ainsley a tip that several politicians were choosing which companies could compete for new environmental projects. By creating narrow requirements in the environmental bills, they eliminated the competition for specific favored companies. This week she was hoping to garner national attention because she just found out several senators had participated in illegal stock purchases based on this insider information—and she could prove it.

After graduating from journalism school six years ago, she'd landed her first job for the D.C. local news network as a research assistant. It was better than being freelance but not by much. She'd worked in a pool of journalists all fighting to find the next story for the producer to include in the daily or nightly news reports. After a run of good luck on local corrupt city legislatures and a news anchor quitting, she'd been promoted to a junior news anchor for the six a.m. report. That was a year ago, and she mostly reported on traffic jams and local puff pieces. But she wanted more. She wanted to report the real news, and her dream was to move up the ranks as a national news correspondent.

To do that, she needed a big break. She had the city's attention after her last three exposé reports, but protecting her source's identity was getting trickier. It wasn't uncommon for other news networks to try to scoop a story, and D.C. was filled with climbers. But the nagging idea that someone involved in the corruption could be trying to shut down her story had the hairs on the back of her neck standing up.

After one last look in her mirror to make sure no one was behind her car, she opened her door and stepped out. Her purse was weighed down by her laptop, and she struggled to get it on her shoulder. A shadow appeared by the back of her car. Gripping a new canister of mace she bought recently, she peered into the dimly lit space. Hoping to stall them, she screamed as she lifted the canister and prayed it was facing the stranger.

"Don't shoot," the voice of her intern, Mark, screeched, and the coffee cup he was holding went flying into the air, crashing down on the roof of the car next to hers.

"Dang it, Mark. Don't sneak up on me like that in a dark garage. Are you crazy?"

He held his hands to his chest and breathed heavily.

"You told me to meet you at five."

"In the office, not in the garage like a stalker. How'd you even know I was here?"

Still heaving to catch his breath, he stood up straighter with his trusty notepad clutched to his side.

"I have the find my phone app linked to your phone, so I can always find you." He picked up the now empty coffee cup and lid off the other car and held it out away from his crisply ironed suit.

She couldn't help but be impressed and creeped out with his ability to locate her. "Good thinking. Let's go." She pushed him forward to move out into the garage toward the elevator. "I just got the next big piece of the puzzle, and I want to craft my monologue before it's time to go on air."

Mark whooped. "You have forty-seven minutes." He

threw away the empty cup before they stepped into the elevator.

"Great. We'll need more coffee."

After locking herself in a small office on the fringe of the network's bullpen, Ainsley crafted up her lines for the six o'clock news report. It wasn't really her office, but she'd snuck in and taken it over after the previous anchor quit. There was a huge whiteboard hanging on one wall that outlined the story she'd been covering for weeks. Each new piece of information was added to the board so she could visualize the scheme as it took shape. Although the story had fallen into her lap, finding another source had taken a lot of effort. She attended a dozen events the political crowd in D.C. frequented and made a list of every senator and their aides that could be involved in the environmentally geared bills. Finally she found someone with connections to the Senate Environmental Quality committee, and they spilled all the tea. An off-the-record chat with a jaded aide whose idealism was being crushed by political infighting and wealthy senators more worried about getting political wins than doing good.

Her source was leaving D.C., unable to stomach the mire of national politics, but provided the specific names of the companies and the bills moving through the Senate that would make those companies worth a lot of money. Whoever owned those companies, or their stocks, were going to get filthy rich. Everything fell under the umbrella of a green movement on the Hill. Being environmentally conscious was having a revival referred to as the Green is Good batch of bills. Which, by all accounts was great, but the corruption could destroy all the good the environmentally friendly bills could do.

She wasn't prepared to name specific politicians involved yet, and was hoping she wouldn't need to. As soon as she plastered the names of the companies involved on the screen and the amounts of money being made daily on stock trades, it would send up a red flag. The media and Senate watch dogs would look into who owned those companies and who was making the most money. But first, she needed to do a little more research to prove the companies were frauds, new LLCs with no staff or previous contracts. And ideally, she was hoping her research would pinpoint the ringleader.

Breaking her concentration, the station's receptionist's voice crackled through the intercom on her desk phone.

"Nash here," Ainsley called out to the young woman who sounded as nervous as a virgin on her wedding night.

"Ms. Nash, there's an officer here to see you?"

Ainsley huffed.

"I don't have time for police tips tonight. Can you just take down his number for me?"

"He's already on his way back," the receptionist warned.

Ainsley's eyes shot up to look through the glass window of her small office and watched a large man, dressed in all black, stalking through the reporter bullpen. The sounds of the furious typing and journalists calling sources fell to a whisper as every eye watched him navigate the furniture that looked like toys next to him. His head towered over the cubicles, and most of the men standing were dwarfed by his broad shoulders.

As he cleared the workspace, she could see a weapon

strapped to his right thigh, a badge on his belt, and police patches on his shirt and shoulders. With tawny brown hair and a chiseled jaw, she could tell the man was used to getting a lot of attention. Lucky for her, he stopped in the doorway to her office.

"Ms. Nash?" he asked.

His tone had the air of authority that indicated he already knew who she was. With deep green eyes, he scanned her from head to toe observationally.

"It depends. Who are you?"

She let her eyes run up and down his figure again to prove he wasn't intimidating her, even as a shiver of awareness ran over her bare arms.

"Sergeant Maguire. I'm with the D.C. Metro Emergency Response Team."

"That's a mouthful. What can I do for you, Sergeant?" she said, unable to stop from smiling at the scowl on his gorgeous face.

"Your father called in a favor, and I've been assigned to protect you this evening."

There was a hint of displeasure rolling off of him, but his tone remained neutral.

"Protect me? From what? The six o'clock rating spike I'm chasing on a Friday night?"

The man took a step forward, and his full lips spread in a big, dazzling-but-forced smile, "May I?" He gestured toward the interior of her office.

It would be surprising to find a woman alive who could deny him anything, she thought, as she spotted a faint dimple in his left cheek.

"Of course, Sergeant, please come in." She gestured for him to sit in the one armchair across from her desk where she leaned back on the edge.

"Can you tell me about the threats you've been experiencing?"

The man sat stiffly in the armchair with a pen and a small notebook he retrieved from one of the pockets in his tactical pants. His broad shoulders took over the wall behind him.

"I'm sorry, but I think you have been misinformed. I haven't received any threats. Least of all, one that requires the head of a SWAT team to protect me. Not that I mind your attention, but I think someone is playing a prank on you—or me."

His eyes were like a mood ring that changed based on his emotions. His charming smile was gone, and his now dark, emerald-green eyes studied her before he took a deep breath.

"Ms. Nash, I'm not in the habit of being pranked, and I doubt very much my captain would send me on a wild goose chase for funsies. So if you could please tell me what kind of a threat I need to be watching out for, then we'll get along just fine."

She was tempted to laugh, but he seemed serious and annoyed with her.

"Look, I'm not holding back. I really haven't had any threats."

"Maybe a source went wrong. Perhaps another socialite on the circuit is jealous you wore the same dress to a charity event—or maybe an ex-boyfriend? If you choose not to clue me in, then I'll need to treat anyone that comes near you as a threat. Which will result in shutting down the set until my SWAT team can screen everyone to be sure there is no threat here."

His face was completely impassive with no hint of amusement, and she fought her desire to smile. For some reason, riling this man up was more tempting than every minute in her last relationship.

"SWAT team?" A nervous laugh escaped, and she cringed at the wave of annoyance that ran over the sergeant's face.

He took a deep breath.

"Look, Sergeant, I didn't phone any police captain about any threat, because there isn't one. I can handle ex-boyfriends, and I don't hang out with socialites. Come to think of it, I don't appreciate the implication that I'm some sort of princess making false claims to lure a muscle-bound SWAT team here. That is not my idea of fun, not by a long shot." She realized that may not be completely honest because she did oddly enjoy this exchange. "Why don't you call this captain of yours and tell him he has been misinformed."

"She."

"What?"

"My captain is a she."

"Well, whoever she is, she is wrong."

The sergeant stood with his lips pressed together in a grimace.

"Fine, we can play it this way. Just remember, you were warned."

Before she could respond, her intern Mark opened the

door with two fresh coffees and his hands full of papers.

"Stop right there," the sergeant said in a menacing calm voice, and Mark yelped, dropping the coffee while his hands flew in the air and notes sprinkled down on the now spilled coffee.

"What the hell?" She jumped up to protect Mark, but the sergeant was already on him, patting him down. She was surprised at how fast he could move his large, ripped body.

"Who are you, and what do you do here?" the sergeant said.

Mark stood with his hands up high. "I'm Mark, Ms. Nash's intern. I get coffee, research, powder noses, and help her pick out shoes."

"Fascinating. Have you noticed anything strange lately? Unexpected visitors, packages, phone calls?"

Mark looked from Ainsley to the sergeant. "Besides you, sir?"

"Enough. You can't just come in here and harass the staff based on some bogus tip."

"On the contrary, it's called police work, and Captain Sullivan is not the type to provide a bogus tip to the head of her SWAT team. But what I can do is this, all night long. I will jack up anyone who comes within five feet of you. I don't get paid to be nice. I get paid to protect you."

"Outstanding," Mark breathed, clearly already enthralled by the sergeant's domineering technique.

Mark bent down to pick up the coffee-stained papers and tossed the spilled coffee in the trash.

"Uhhhh, Mark, go get yourself another coffee, please. I'll meet you on set," Ainsley said.

"No, you won't. Not until I clear everyone on set."

Mark stood like a deer in headlights looking back and forth between them.

"Go," she said, giving Mark a little push out of her office before slamming the door closed behind him.

"You barge in here giving orders and making a mess, expecting me to just follow orders. Well, newsflash, I don't report to you. Call your captain now."

Her voice was higher than she intended, but she wasn't accustomed to such a large masculine man bossing her around. No matter how attractive he was, it was starting to piss her off.

"Gladly."

He pulled out his phone and put the call on speaker. The captain picked up on the first ring.

"Sully, I'm with the uncooperative subject, and she doesn't seem to know anything about any threats. Can I treat her as a hostile protectee? Maybe just stow her in a secure safe house for the night."

"Take me off speaker, sergeant," a woman's assertive voice sounded clear over the phone.

He did as commanded, and Ainsley couldn't hear the rest of the very short conversation. Annoyed, she walked behind her desk and dug her cell phone out of her purse. She knew the one person who was likely behind this and who could outrank the sergeant and his captain.

The phone only rang once.

"Dad, do you have any idea why D.C. Metro SWAT would think I require a protection detail?"

The sergeant ended his call and stared her in the eyes until she put the call on speakerphone. He had mastered the art of commanding with his eyes, and she wondered if they taught that in police school.

"Ainsley, it's nice of you to finally return one of my calls."

"Please don't tell me this is an attempt to manipulate me into doing what you want. Not even you would stoop this low," she said.

"I'd rather not talk about this over the phone. I've tried to reach you all week, and you ignored my assistant when he stopped by your place last night."

"I can't believe you would make up some false threat, waste the police department's time, all in an attempt to get my attention. This is a gross misuse of power, not to mention a waste of taxpayers' money and pathetic."

"Enough, Ainsley. You will allow the police to provide you protection and you will meet with me tonight and that is final." Her dad's stern tone reminded her of the time she took his new sports car for a joyride when she was sixteen.

She saw red, her skin heated, and annoyance filled her gut like it usually did when she spoke to her pompous father. Before she could form a response, Rory stood and leaned over the phone to speak.

"Senator Nash, this is Sergeant Rory Maguire with the D.C. Metro Emergency Response Team. What time and where should I bring your daughter for the meeting?" He raised his hand before she could argue.

"My office, seven o'clock."

Annoyed, she walked toward the window and pushed her fingers on her temple, willing her emotions to stay in check as the frustration of the situation settled over her.

"Is there an agent on your detail I should coordinate with?"

She vaguely heard her father respond before he hung up.

"I don't need a SWAT team to babysit me. You can leave, sergeant," she said over her shoulder and continued to stare out the window, not seeing anything.

"It doesn't work that way, Ms. Nash. I'm afraid we're stuck with each other until I can prove there's no threat."

She turned to face him, surprised to see the regret on his face mixed with pity.

"I go on air in ten minutes, and then we can argue about why I'm not going to let my father dictate to me where to go on any given night."

"Ms. Nash, if the senator's team believes there's a viable threat, it's worth a meeting to find out why. Then we'll know what to look out for or not. The sooner I can prove there is no threat to you, the sooner I can get out of your hair. No offense, but pulling a protection detail isn't exactly why I got into law enforcement."

She took a deep breath but didn't let her shoulders hang in complete defeat. She could see Mark through the glass wall of her office, tapping his watch and holding her coffee.

"Fine, I'll play by your rules for one meeting with my father's security detail, and then we go our separate ways." She grabbed her blazer and opened the door. "Can you please not frisk everyone on set?"

"We'll see," he said.

"Most of them will only enjoy it, and you're going to be distracting enough as it is."

She couldn't help but smile at the look of surprise on his face that someone would enjoy being frisked. She wouldn't mind if he needed to practice on her. The man was like every alpha male ever portrayed in a cop movie: broad shoulders, flirty eyes, and muscles everywhere.

Chapter Three

ONCE THEY WERE on the sound stage, Rory tried to lurk in the shadows while remaining within arm's length of Ainsley. But the room was buzzing with activity, bright lights, cords everywhere, and people with headphones barking out orders. He couldn't believe all this was necessary. He watched as her hair was sprayed and curled, and her lips slathered with bright red lipstick before she slid her petite feet out of her sneakers and into four-inch heels.

She smiled and spoke kindly to everyone and remained calm as someone with a clipboard called out the time. Her assistant poured her coffee into a mug with the station emblem on it, and she whispered something in his ear before pointing to where Rory stood.

"Sergeant, do you want water or coffee? Ms. Nash suggested you may need to stay hydrated," Mark stammered, looking at Rory's hand gripping his thigh rig where his service weapon sat.

"Water would be great, thanks, Mark. Sorry about the shakedown earlier."

"No problem, sir."

Mark scurried off while Rory stood watching Ainsley. Her long legs were crossed and canted to the side of the tall table where she sat. The lights were dimmed but still high-lighted her beauty. Maybe it wouldn't be so bad doing protection for such an attractive woman for a day or two. He assumed she had a boyfriend that wouldn't like a police detail being underfoot, but that was too bad. Orders were orders. Clearly, he had been working too much if a pretty face could trick him into looking forward to this assignment.

Reappearing with an eager smile, Mark handed him a bottle of water before he took up the space next to him. He could feel Mark's eyes on him as he proceeded to cross his arms over his clipboard and spread his feet wide, copying Rory's stance.

He instantly regretted grinning when Ainsley looked up and caught his humor. A faint smirk passed her lips before another young man placed a mic on her neckline, and Rory fought the urge to punch the guy. Granted, he was supposed to protect her, but he doubted he could force any man to not enjoy being close enough to touch her smooth tan skin. Gulping down his water, he watched and waited.

"It's go time," Mark whispered.

Rory watched as the lights turned up several notches, and Ainsley faced the camera in front of her.

"Five, four, three, two…" A man pointed to Ainsley, and she launched into a monologue on the highlights of the latest news in D.C.. Clips of video on the recent rise in homeless found throughout the district ran on the large screens behind her. This was followed by a short commercial break in which her team re-powdered her already perfect face and fluffed her hair. Back on air, she launched into details of her headline story.

She'd been covering an exposé on shady government contracts on the hill and had new evidence to link favored companies and stock trades. Her demeanor shifted, and her excitement over this story was obvious. She provided more details to the viewers, and a link chart took over the screen behind her. In the center of the chart was an empty circle. She reviewed the facts known but didn't lead people on with her personal thoughts or assessment. She set up the details for the viewers to determine who had the most to gain from bills that all but named specific companies to fulfill the newly required environmentally safe work.

He wondered if Ainsley knew who was behind the scheme and assumed this had something to do with her father's concerns. Was Senator Nash involved? Would she out her father for the truth to be out?

In her final comments, a graphic outlining the billions that could be made popped up on the screens. The names of the specific companies appeared in bold colors. These firms were dominating the market on environmental materials, and there was a clear uptick in stock trades for those companies.

"The new face of organized crime is hidden in stock purchases and being run by lawmakers, making it nearly impossible for everyday citizens to determine who to trust. The trail is murky, but I've got your back, D.C.. Tune in for more updates next week," she said to the camera with no hint of a smile.

The lights dimmed, and someone yelled, "We're off air."

Rory was riveted. She commanded attention the entire time, and not because of her irrefutable beauty. When she faced the camera, there was so much more. She was compelling and articulate without talking down to average American viewers. Even more, she was passionate about the news, and he couldn't help but be impressed.

She pulled her dark hair up off her shoulders into a swirl piled on top of her head as her assistant retrieved the mic off her collar. Smiling, she kicked off the heels before picking them up and sliding on her sneakers again. Mark was right by her side retrieving her discarded heels, and the blazer she was quick to shed.

"You'll freeze outside with just that on," Rory warned, as he stepped close to her and ignored all the looks he was getting from her colleagues. It was early April, and the temps were still in the forties once the sun went down.

"I have a coat in my office. It's just so hot under those lights. I need to cool off."

He nodded and followed her back to her office while simultaneously trying to get every door and check every hallway before she moved. Mark blathered while complimenting her presence on air.

It was only half-past six, and Rory was anxious to meet up with the senator's security team to learn more about the alleged threat.

"We need to get going. We'll take my car," he said, waiting outside her office door. He could tell she wanted to argue, but she pressed her pert lips together, grabbed her bag and coat, and told Mark he was done for the night.

"I'll see you Monday, Ms. Nash, unless you need me this weekend?" Mark said, sounding disappointed.

"Enjoy the weekend and do something I wouldn't do,"

she called, walking toward him out of her office, clearly expecting Rory to follow, which he did.

"Do you always have to wear all that gear?" she said.

"You mean my uniform? Yes. Do you always have to wear all that makeup?"

"You mean my uniform in a world that expects women to look like beauty queens? Yes, unfortunately, I do."

"I doubt you need that much makeup for the camera to love you, but you tell yourself whatever you need to."

"I bet you don't need that many bullets to stop a jay-walker."

Rory huffed. He wasn't about to get into an argument with the senator's daughter on how many rounds an officer needed for the myriad of situations they could find themselves in. Once they were inside the elevator, he stood in front of her and pressed the garage level where he'd parked. When the doors chimed, she moved to go in front of him, and he placed his arm up to stop her.

"I get you don't think you need me, but until we're sure, will you just let me play bodyguard? Please?"

As much as it cost him to ask, it deflated her argument enough to let him win that round. She waited for him to exit and look around the immediate area before he gripped her arm to escort her to his car, listening and moving swiftly.

"This is so extra," she said.

"Excuse me?"

"My father is being a control freak, and this little stunt is his latest attempt to bend me to his will. I'm not interested in being a glossy feature of his campaign or aspirations for the White House. So he's punishing me."

"You don't get along with your dad?"

"None of your business," she snapped as she got into his car while he held her door open.

"Maybe." Rory closed her door.

He stayed quiet the rest of the drive toward the Capitol building where they were due to meet the senator's chief of staff and his security detail to be briefed on the possible threat. As he pulled toward the VIP security entrance, his phone began to go off with multiple texts.

Hostage standoff. You still babysitting? a message from Jake read.

"Damn it," he muttered.

"Are you getting called away? That sounds about right. Just in time to dump me with my manipulative father."

"No, I'm just missing a real crime in progress, but my team can manage."

When they stopped behind several cars at the first security checkpoint, he took the opportunity to study her demeanor. It was clear she wasn't excited to see her father. She'd wiped off all her makeup with whatever she'd been pulling out of her bag. There was a smattering of freckles on the bridge of her nose and cheeks that only made her more attractive. If that was possible. The red lipstick was replaced with clear gloss, and her brown eyes looked like amber in the fading sun that shone into the front windshield.

"I was right," he said before he could stop himself.

"About what?" she snapped, narrowing her eyes on him.

She was being handled and was pissed and he didn't blame her. At the same time, her father thought there was a great enough threat to call in a favor to the D.C. SWAT

Team but not tell her what it was.

"You didn't need the makeup."

Her pouty lips parted slightly with surprise at the implied compliment, but he looked away to focus on the slalomed entrance into the garage under the rotunda. The last thing he needed was his protectee getting offended or accusing him of hitting on her.

Chapter Four

AINSLEY WATCHED AS the uniformed officers checked Sergeant Maguire's credentials before ushering them through the hallways in the underbelly of the Capitol building. The size and confusion of the building's maze of hallways with intricate marble details never disappointed. The summer before her freshman year of college, when her dad first took office as a senator, she had been in awe. Now she knew the truth behind the power of politics. Working as a journalist in D.C. provided her an inside look at how often politicians could change their stance on an issue based on pressure from other more powerful senators, extortion, or worse.

The doorway to her father's office was marked only by the gleaming wood which hinted that someone important sat beyond the stark white hallway. Behind this door lay some of the largest office space in the building, held for decades by the senior senator from New York State. Rory had stayed close to her the entire walk with his hand a breath away from her back. She could feel the heat as if he branded her with his touch, when in reality, he only briefly touched her now as she stopped short to wait for the secretary to allow entrance into her father's suite of rooms. Once they were buzzed through, the Capitol officers peeled off. She hoped Rory was paying attention because she'd been too distracted by him to remember how to get back to their car.

Stepping onto the plush, thick blue carpet in the foyer of her father's office, his long-time secretary met them like a castle sentry.

"Ms. Nash, your father is in a meeting. If you and your guest don't mind waiting here." Her father's secretary ushered them into a small anteroom.

In reality, it was a control room for visitors that was useful to politicians when they didn't want whoever they were meeting with to run into other guests.

Ainsley rolled her eyes as she plopped into a stiff leather armchair.

"As expected, now we wait."

Rory stood near the door taking in his surroundings, giving her a prime opportunity to study him. He was still equal parts drop-dead gorgeous and serious. Totally sexy.

"I've never been inside the Capitol before. Seems odd, considering I grew up in the area."

"You're from D.C.? I didn't think anyone was ever actually from this city."

"Third generation."

Before she could delve into his background, a man in a rumpled suit opened the door to the holding room they were in and barked "This way," before walking away.

She felt Rory's eyes on her, looking for information on the man.

"Jenkins is my father's chief of staff. He's a snake, so watch out," Ainsley whispered as he held the door open for her.

She couldn't help but like the idea of having his focused attention and eyes on her regularly.

The large burgundy door behind the secretary was open now, and she followed Jenkins inside.

"Let's make this quick, Dad. I have plans tonight," Ainsley said. She knew better than to let her father think he was running this show, even though he was.

Her father sat behind his desk in a tailored navy suit and red power tie. His blue eyes wrinkled on the edges, and his previously blonde hair was now a whitish gray that only made him look more distinguished. He had been dubbed one of the most attractive politicians in the Senate when he was first elected ten years ago, and likely remained on that list. Although she had her mother's darker Italian features, she had the same bone structure as her dad, with pronounced cheekbones and a proud brow.

"Hello, darling. It's nice to see you too. I'm sorry, but your plans may need to be changed." Her father stood and walked around his majestic desk to kiss her on each side of her cheeks, and his hands settled on her upper arms before he pulled her in for a hug.

His familiar scent and warm embrace were comforting, but she remained stiff.

In truth, she'd been pissed for years that her father put his family second her entire life. First, with his business in New York, then his political career. For as long as she could remember, her parents lived separate lives, and she and her sister were stuck in the middle.

"Why don't we let Sergeant Maguire decide if this alleged threat is worth his time," Ainsley said, ushering to the large man that stood just inside the doorway observing them.

Rory's eyes were on her when she spoke but moved to meet her father's head-on. Although her father was tall, his height didn't match Rory's or his muscular size. Her dad walked back around his desk and sat down without properly greeting Rory by shaking his hand. Something seemed off. Her dad usually pretended not to be so bossy, but this evening, he was being openly obstinate and controlling.

"There is no question of if the threat is real or if you'll have protection," her father said in his stern tone. "The chief of D.C. Metro has already agreed to provide around-the-clock protection. If Mr. Maguire refuses his assignment, I'm sure that won't reflect well on his career, and someone will replace him."

Her father looked at Jenkins with some unsaid message.

"Dad, we need to know what the threat is. How could anyone be expected to provide protection when they don't even know the source of the threat?"

"No, he needs to watch you and make sure you aren't hurt. It's quite simple." Her father's tone was even, but it was clear he expected his orders to be followed.

Ainsley looked from her father's stubborn face to Rory who remained impassive. Studying her father again a chill ran down her spine. His brow was furrowed, and his shoulders were cinched up around his neck; he was worried. Meanwhile, Jenkins stood to the side of her father's desk looking smug before handing Ainsley a picture of a man with a cheesy smile plastered on his fake tan face.

"Clark, are you telling me your protégé, the junior senator from New York, is the threat? You can't be serious."

Ainsley stood and handed Rory the picture.

"No, Clark was attacked yesterday. He was out on his morning run and was found unconscious in the park. Beat up. He's still in the hospital," Jenkins said in a tone that implied he was frustrated to have to spell things out for them.

Unease washed over her, remembering what her source had said about the insider trading scheme. There were reports of someone getting greedy, and threats being made. But she couldn't be sure this event was linked to her story. D.C. was a big city with a high crime rate.

"I'm sorry for the senator, but how is this related to why you think I need protection?" Ainsley asked.

"Because whoever did this may target your father next," Jenkins said.

"And because the senator has a protective detail already, you're worried his family is a more vulnerable target?" Rory said.

Her father narrowed his eyes on Rory. "Exactly. So you see, Ainsley, you need to cooperate and allow Mr. Maguire to protect you, or you can go stay with your mother and sister in Italy."

"Moving to Amalfi indefinitely is out of the question."

"Then it would appear Mr. Maguire is your only option," her father said.

"It's sergeant, Dad. At least use his proper title," Ainsley said, annoyed.

Her father shook his head absentmindedly, "Of course, Sergeant Maguire."

"What are your leads on the attackers? Why would you assume it was political and Senator Nash is also in danger? How do you know it wasn't just random?" Rory said.

He stood, challenging her father, and ignoring Jenkins, as if it was the normal course of action. Her father sat back against his chair with the hint of a smirk while he unclenched his fist and studied Rory.

"I met your father a few times when I arrived in D.C., Commissioner Maguire—he was very well respected. Your captain assures me you're the best SWAT officer for the job, to protect Ainsley," her father said.

"Perhaps a new perspective could help the investigation, senator," Rory replied.

Her father's tired face broke into a genuine smile. Rory wasn't going to be deterred and he wasn't intimidated to learn her father spoke to his captain. She suspected he had his own powerful connections within D.C. if his father was the police commissioner.

"Access to details in the investigation would require special security clearances, which you lack," Jenkins said, interrupting.

Instead of responding to Jenkins, Rory addressed her father directly.

"Sir, I understand there are sensitivities in this situation, but the more I know, the better prepared I'll be to protect your daughter against any threat," Rory said.

She couldn't help but admire his calm confidence.

"All that may be true, but we can't risk this information hitting the press. We can't share any information at this time."

Her father sighed, and she noticed, for the first time, circles under his eyes.

"You won't tell us more about the threat because you're afraid I'll use it as a story?" Ainsley said as disappointment erupted through her body. "Not only does that tell me you're up to your eyeballs in something career-ending, but you're willing to risk my safety for the truth not to come out?" Ainsley stood to face off with her father.

"You don't know what you're talking about, Ainsley, and you're better off not knowing. I wish you could trust I only have your best interests at heart, but nevertheless, this is how it is going to be."

His fatigue was visible on his handsome face, causing him to look older than she ever remembered him looking.

"Fine, but I'm not going to sit at home and twiddle my thumbs because some political deal you've made has gone wrong. I'm going to start digging. So you better get your house in order and figure out a solution. And if anything happens to mom or Amelia, you'll have more than hell to pay."

"Your grandfather will be handling their protection, and as you know, the compound is massive and difficult to get to. I'm insulted that you assume I'm at fault in all of this."

"How could I not since you're the one forcing me into the situation without any details?"

"I'm sure Officer Maguire can enlighten you about the kind of people that like to take the law into their own hands."

Ainsley turned to look up at Rory. "We're better off looking for clues ourselves. They aren't going to tell us anything."

Rory grimaced. "Then I have to assume the worst, which means I'll need more resources to protect you."

Ainsley huffed and walked toward the door. "I'm not going to live in a safe house," she called out over her shoulder as she walked to open the heavy door.

Rory was there in two strides to catch up to her and open the door for her. His hand settled on her lower back.

"Please let me walk through any doorways first, Ms. Nash," he said in a polite but still curt tone.

Feeling the warmth and pressure of his hand through the fabric of her dress on her lower back pushed goosebumps to cover her arms under her coat. With a deep exhale, she conceded and gestured toward the doorway for him to go first.

"Be safe, Ainsley, and please listen to Officer Maguire," her father called.

She stopped in her tracks and faced her father again.

"Sergeant, Dad. His title is sergeant. He's the head of a SWAT team, for goodness sakes." She stalked out.

She was surprised to see Rory grinning as he held the door to exit her father's office.

"Why are you laughing? None of this seems very humorous to me."

She was so mad she didn't notice how fast she was walking until she almost ran into another person coming around a corner, headed their way. Rory easily intercepted her by placing a hand on her elbow and blocking her from running into the young woman who looked terrified that she could be someone important.

"I agree this situation isn't funny but hearing you correct your father twice about my rank was enjoyable. For a man who called in a favor to have me in charge of your protection, you would think he'd get my rank correct."

"I agree, he seemed very distracted. Speaking of, didn't your captain want more details on why you were being sidelined for protection?"

"I suspect this order trickled down from the top. If your dad did speak with my captain, I doubt she managed to get any more details than us, and she wouldn't push."

"Maybe you can ask around," she said.

"Maybe."

They walked the rest of the way in silence. Was Rory always so introspective or was this his on-duty persona? If they were going to be stuck spending time together, she may as well try to get to know him. Besides being extremely attractive, she got the feeling he was the kind of man with layers. Tough and brute strength on the outside but maybe soft and tender beyond his walls?

Chapter Five

DRIVING AINSLEY OFF the congressional compound, Rory remained quiet and made his way out of D.C.. He ran her name in a police database to find her address, assuming she would want to collect a few things before they found a suitable safe house location for her.

"Where are we going?" she asked.

"Your residence, so you can pack a few things."

"How do you know where I live? And I'm not packing anything. I'm not living out of my suitcase because my father is in bed with corrupt thugs. I understand this puts you in a difficult position, but I'm staying in my condo."

"Ms. Nash."

"Call me Ainsley."

"Ainsley, I can't provide sufficient protection for you alone against an unknown threat. I need a team, and we draw attention. It's not safe to stay at your place. Anyone can Google you and find out where you live."

"No, they can't. I'm very careful about privacy measures. My building has a doorman, I purchased my home using an LLC, and my mail is delivered to a P.O. box. How did you find my address?"

"I ran your name in our computer, and it spit out your

address off Arlington Blvd."

She smiled. "Oh, okay. Let's go there."

He didn't like the sound of humor in her voice but didn't feel like arguing. Fifteen minutes later, when he was directed to pull into a specialty wine store named Amalfi's Vine, he realized he'd been had.

"You use a business address for your driver's license? That's illegal."

"It's my grandfather's shop, and they wouldn't let me use the P.O. box."

"It's still not your residence."

"Are you going to arrest me? Maybe frisk me like you did to Mark?"

He tried to look into her hazel eyes, but the space between them in his SUV was too dark. Her tone was playful, but he couldn't help but wonder if she was toying with him. There was no denying she was a desirable woman, but he wasn't going to be distracted from his duty to protect her.

"No, I'm not going to frisk you. But if you don't tell me where you live, you'll be stuck wearing those clothes to bed. We'll have to sleep on cots in the SWAT team office, where I doubt you'll enjoy a restful night's sleep, between emergency calls, shift work, and the gym."

"Take a right out of the parking lot and head north on Route 1."

He did as directed and was pleasantly surprised twenty minutes later when they pulled into a garage along the Potomac River under a small six-story building. Compared to some of the large, towering condo buildings along the water, hers was more manageable from a protective standpoint. He was open to letting her stay at her place if he was sure he could secure the location.

Pulling into a visitor parking spot, he turned off the car. Shooting his arm out in front of her, he held her back from opening her door.

"Humor me, please."

She huffed but sat back.

"Okay. You're right. For all I know, this threat is real, and it's stupid to ignore it and put us both in harm's way, just to spite my domineering father."

"Good. So who knows where you live?" he asked before exiting the car.

"My mom and sister have been here. A few friends that aren't involved in politics or journalism. I don't have any bills in my name because there are psychos out there."

"Like crazy fans?" he asked.

"Sort of. People fixate on the personalities they see on TV and then get curious about their real lives. Some people will invade your privacy, so I just put everything in the business name. My mom's family owns the specialty wine shop, so it's just easier."

"Okay, can you give me your keys, please? I'm going to go take a look and make sure nothing has been tampered with while you wait here."

"You're going to leave me alone? Won't that defeat the purpose of having you as my shadow?"

Just then another blacked-out SUV pulled up beside his.

"My teammate is going to sit with you while I make sure everything is secure."

Ainsley leaned forward to look at the darkened windows,

unable to see who was in the car, and waved before sitting back.

"Can you leave me a gun?"

"No."

"Party pooper."

His laugh filled the truck, surprising them both. Ainsley looked like a child that figured out a magic trick by getting him to laugh.

"Ah, so you do have a sense of humor," she said as he opened his car door and exited.

"Yes, but I'm surprised you do after today. Keep the doors locked until I get back," he ordered.

"Yes, sir." She mocked him by saluting before handing him her keys.

All humor left when her hand brushed his; the feel of her delicate fingers in his palm sparked a current through him. A simple touch had him wondering if her skin was that soft in other places.

Grunting, he locked the door and shut it, then walked around to speak to Jake.

"Looks like you're already in over your head. You need me to take the night shift?"

"No chance. She's not enthused to have a protective detail, and her father wouldn't tell us much. Senator Nash's junior senator and protégé was attacked a few days ago, sounds like they think it was a message for the senator."

"I heard about it this evening at roll call. I take it wasn't a random act of violence?" Jake said.

"Senator Nash is afraid whatever the junior senator was involved in will get leaked to the press, so they wouldn't give us any more details."

"And since his little princess is the press, we're in the dark."

"Looks like it."

"Alright, you're okay with using her place, or should we get a hotel suite?"

"I need to confirm how many units are on her floor. She's not a fan of lying low in a safe house, and it's possible we can make this work."

"Agreed. It's small. Only one vehicle entrance," Jake said.

"We'll need to decide how many guys on the team to bring into shifts, then I can plot out a rotation."

Jake nodded. "Sounds like this isn't going to be a short assignment."

"No, it doesn't. The senator and his chief of staff were very cagey."

"I bet Ms. Nash is already contacting her sources," Jake said.

"Just keep your head on a swivel while I make sure her place is clear."

Rory looked into his SUV where Ainsley sat but could barely make out her figure in the dimly lit garage.

Walking into the building, he was met with sleek modern doors, marble details in the hallway, and a desk where a concierge sat like a sentry to the elevators. Pulling out his police credentials, he stopped in front of the high counter, where an elderly man sat eyeing him.

"You're out of your jurisdiction, Sergeant," the man said, standing.

"Technically, I have police authority in the tri-state area,

Stanley." He read the man's name on the gold tag buttoned to his blazer.

The man studied his D.C. Metro credentials before waving them off for Rory to put away.

"How may I help you, Sergeant?"

"For starters, can you give me an overview of the shifts? How many concierges rotate each day? Have there been any odd guests lately?"

Stanley rattled off the rotation and gave Rory several names, each of the staff who worked for the building, hired by the housing board.

"And my second question."

"It's funny you should arrive tonight because there was a car I noticed on my afternoon rounds. When we each take over our shift, we walk around the building, check the waterfront for any broken glass or homeless people, and cars in the garage that don't belong to a resident."

"And?"

"At the start of my shift at two pm, a man was standing along the water, smoking a cigarette, just staring up at the building. I also noticed a black car parked across from the parking garage."

"It's metered parking over there. I noticed." Rory said.

"Indeed, much as the housing board tries to fight the city, anyone can park there as long as they feed the meter."

"Anyone sitting in the car?"

"No, sir, and the man smoking was average height, average everything. He turned away to look at the water as I passed."

"Good eye, Stanley. I hope I can count on you and the

other staff to keep your eyes peeled. We'll have several officers on twenty-four-hour shifts with Ms. Nash indefinitely, one additional officer in the garage, and perhaps another patrolling the area."

"Very good, sir. I hope you're as tough as you look. Ms. Ainsley is my favorite resident. I'd hate to have to blame you if something happened to her."

"I'll do my best, but I'd appreciate updates, no matter how small, on any changes in the routine on the premises."

"Done."

"I'm going to go up and confirm her condo is safe before she gets home. She gave me her key," Rory said, holding up the keys.

Stanley hit a button, and an elevator door opened. "Penthouse, unit number two. Turn left when you exit the elevator."

"Thanks." Rory entered the elevator, and Stanley sat back down.

Was Ainsley the doorman's favorite because she was the most beautiful resident or the most friendly? Based on the way she treated her colleagues at the network, it surprised him to think she may be both.

Once on the sixth floor, Rory followed the directions and didn't see any signs of entry. The door was locked, but the alarm was off. Making his way through the large two-bedroom condo was fast. Beyond the foyer was a large kitchen and a living room. Open concept with wood floors, one wall of sliding doors that led to a veranda running along the length of the condo. Down a short hallway were two bedrooms. He checked each bathroom and all the closets but found no signs of disturbance. The glass sliding doors were not locked, and he would have to talk to her about making a few changes in her routine.

Five minutes later, he walked back into the garage to find Jake sitting in Rory's driver's seat next to Ainsley.

Opening the door on Jake's side, he pinned Ainsley with a stare. "I thought I told you not to unlock the doors," Rory said with more malice than he'd intended.

"I got bored and thought it would be prudent to meet a man that is being saddled with protecting me. I assume you won't be with me every minute, so Jake will likely also get to play shadow over the next few days."

Jake smiled and made no move to exit the car.

"We'll see," Rory said, frustrated that he was annoyed.

Jake laughed as Rory opened the back of the SUV and grabbed a bag he left packed for nights when his shift ran long and he didn't make it home. He walked around to the passenger's side and opened the door.

"Concierge rotates at ten. You can relieve me at midnight," Rory said to Jake.

Jake nodded. "Sounds good. We'll be as quiet as we can, Ms. Nash, but try not to be startled if I'm in your condo when you wake up." Jake winked at her before exiting the car and closing the door.

Ainsley laughed, and Rory rolled his eyes.

"A girl could do much worse than having you two for company on a Friday night, but what if I'm expecting someone, or have plans?"

Rory pinned her with his eyes, and she had the gall to flutter her lashes back at him with a sly smile.

"Cancel them."

She squinted and stared back as if she were going to challenge him but surprised him by shrugging.

"Fine. May I exit the vehicle, Sergeant?"

"Hang on."

He reached over her lap for the keys in the ignition and got a whiff of her earthy, sweet scent.

Her breath hitched as his head ducked inside the truck, even though there was plenty of space in front of her seat. He caught a glimpse of her bare thighs and felt his pulse quicken, before pulling back out of her space and pocketing the keys.

"I could get used to all this attention. Better tone down the hero mode a bit, Rory," she said.

Gritting his teeth at the rush of desire he felt when she said his name, he backed up a step. Watching her lean leg muscles flex as she exited the car was torture. But he needed to focus. Closing the door for her he placed one hand on her elbow, while he took another look around the garage. All was quiet.

"When we move from building to car or reverse, stay close and behind me. Always put me between you and any access points. So the entrance to the garage is to our left. You stay to my right. Got it?"

Ainsley nodded and did exactly as directed.

He didn't want to scare her, but she needed a healthy dose of concern for her own safety until this wrapped up.

As they entered the building, an elevator door opened, and Rory stopped her to stand close to the wall and behind him while he waited to see who would exit. Peeking around the corner, he found Stanley at attention and an elderly woman with a small dog.

"It's clear," he said, ushering her to move forward and ignoring the elderly woman's eyes growing big with the look of his SWAT gear and size.

"Good evening, Stanley. Hello, Mrs. Rose," Ainsley said sweetly.

"Oh, hello dear. Is this your new fellow?"

Ainsley smiled. "Yes, this is Rory. This is my downstairs neighbor, Mrs. Rose, and her adorable baby, Annabelle." Ainsley placed her hand on Rory's bicep, and he fought the urge to enjoy it. She pulled him to keep moving toward the elevator, not wanting to stop to chat with her neighbor.

"Good night then, Ms. Ainsley, Mr. Rory," Stanley called.

They entered the elevator as Ainsley smiled, still staying close to him and only breaking away when the doors closed.

"Sorry about that. I think it will be easier if we don't let the neighbors know why you're here," she said by way of excuse.

"So your new fellow or one of his police officer friends will be seen with you nonstop now, and you don't think that will get the neighbors talking?" he challenged.

"I mean, you will get the neighbors talking no matter what, but I've made it clear in the past that I'm very private. I've never had anyone ask about my guests, mostly because I rarely have any."

"Your call. I just think the uniform may out us."

The elevator door pinged open, and Rory gripped Ainsley's arm to stop her from walking out first.

"Force of habit."

Her breath hitched, and he could see her pulse moving faster with the rise and fall of her chest. Her lips were slightly parted, and he almost forgot for a split second that she was his protectee and not waiting for him to kiss her.

Mentally kicking himself, he walked out into the hall first but then waited for her to follow. He unlocked the door in silence and bolted the lock once they were inside.

"So you can have the guest room," she said.

"The couch is fine, not that I'll be getting much sleep tonight."

"Me either." She moved into the kitchen and opened the fridge to pull out a water pitcher and bottle of wine.

"I assume you won't be toasting to my safety with me?" she asked, pulling down one wine glass from an open cabinet.

"Definitely not with wine on duty."

"Okay, well, I'm making tacos, so hopefully you like that." She walked back to her room with her glass of wine, leaving the water pitcher and glass for him on the counter.

She didn't close her door, but he could guess she was probably changing. He couldn't help but wish he had an excuse to stay closer to her and then instantly felt like a creep.

A few minutes passed before she reappeared in cozy-looking gray sweats and a black fitted t-shirt with her dark hair pulled back in a low, long ponytail.

In the living room, he sat in a surprisingly comfortable pink armchair that didn't seem to match Ainsley's tough persona. The entire apartment had light wood floors, white curtains, and soft feminine accents. But it wasn't his job to wonder about her softer side, so he retrieved his work laptop from his bag to distract him from the lure of watching her move around the kitchen. He tried to access the police report on the junior senator's assault but hit a dead end. The files were either restricted or yet to be recorded.

Ainsley began pulling out cutting boards, knives, veggies, and pans. She hit a few buttons on a tablet screen embedded in the wall, and music began to play.

"Is it okay if I play music, or are you trying to work?" she asked while holding a knife and standing at the large white marble counter.

He couldn't help but smile. "You don't need my permission to do anything in your house."

"So I can do whatever I want?"

"Within these walls, I have few restrictions. Don't stand in front of windows for too long and lock your doors at night."

"Even my bedroom door?" she said with a touch of worry.

"Yes, and the front door and sliding glass doors that lead out to the patio."

"But we're on the top floor," she said and began chopping a pepper.

"Better safe than sorry."

"Okay, are you going to sleep in front of my bedroom door?"

"Do you want me to?"

"Maybe. No, I'm just kidding. I'm sorry. I know I've been rude, and you're just doing your job."

"Comes with the territory, but it is easier the more cooperative a protectee is."

"I'll try." She met his eyes before focusing back on chopping.

He remained in the living room, not wanting to crowd her and needing to keep some distance to think. He shot Jake a few texts to see if he knew why he couldn't access the reports on the junior senator's attack he was looking for, and Jake said he'd tried to get a copy. But the incident had been turned over to the Capitol Police, and they didn't always share records with D.C. Metro. It was being managed with a need-to-know policy based on the uniqueness of the crime and the victim's political status.

The smell and sounds of vegetables cooking had Rory's stomach growling, and he wondered if he should ask Jake to order them something. It was always best to keep his routine separate from a protectee. The last time he did protection, he was assigned a pompous millionaire whose wife had gone off the rails, so it wasn't hard. He'd never done protection for a gorgeous woman before.

"Are you single?" Ainsley asked just as he took a sip of water and caught him off guard, causing him to choke down the gulp he'd taken.

"I'm not currently dating anyone, if that's what you mean."

"Me either. The last guy I dated said he had a problem with how independent I am."

"At least he was honest about his shortcomings before you got in too deep."

She looked up from pushing the veggies around.

"I guess you're right. I just wish I would have figured that out sooner. He fooled me for months. Then got nasty when I ended it."

"It takes time to try to convince someone to need you."

"Do you think that's necessary for a relationship to work, to need each other?"

"I'm a thirty-four-year-old bachelor, so I'm not the best person to ask. You told your dad you had plans tonight? Should we expect company?"

He was eager to know if he was going to have to deal with anyone else tonight.

"No, I just said that to ensure my father knew how much he was inconveniencing my life with this stunt. Not that he cares in the least."

He noticed a few family pictures on the bookshelf close by, including one of her with her father when she was little. She was standing in a poofy pink dress, and her father wore a tux and he was smiling down at her. The look on her face was pure pride at about age seven.

"You're not close with your dad, yet he called in a favor so you could have your own police protective detail. Care to fill in those blanks for me?"

"No, it has nothing to do with why you're here," she said, not glancing up.

It probably didn't, but he was still curious why she didn't seem to like her father very much.

"Friday night and no plans but tacos?"

"That sounds like judgment. What were your big Friday night plans, Mr. Bachelor?"

"My shift started at five. Do you have any other plans

this weekend I should know about?" he asked, hoping to change the subject.

Her face froze, and she cringed as she met his eyes.

"I do have an event tomorrow night, a gala. It's for a charity, and I can't cancel. I'm the keynote speaker."

He considered this news. It was better to keep her under a tight lock and key. Conversely, if the event was a controlled environment and he had enough coverage, perhaps it would draw the potential threat out, and they could end this protection detail before it even got going. If someone intended on hurting her to get to her dad, they may not suspect she had a protection team yet.

"I hate to say it, but it depends on the event. Where is it being held? Do you know how many people will attend? Is there security, and will other people have bodyguards?"

Ainsley shook her head and threw what looked like shredded pork into her frying pan, then retrieved a half dozen things from the fridge, sour cream, salsa, guac, lettuce, jalapenos, and chips from a cupboard. He could feel her thinking, and it surprised him how calm she was.

"I'll answer all your questions if you join me over here for dinner."

"You don't have to feed us."

The invitation sounded so simple, and he only had to admit to himself that spending the evening with her was the best offer he'd had in months. It was useless to deny he was attracted to her, but what surprised him more was her interest in him. He'd expected her to be cold and indifferent.

"Well, Jake is on his own, but you're here and you must be hungry. I'm starving." She pulled down two plates and set them on the counter. "Besides, I don't like eating alone."

He stood and walked over to the kitchen. In the last four hours, she made it clear she wasn't the type of person to take no for an answer. So he sat down and enjoyed the best homemade tacos he'd ever had while she answered all his questions.

"You know, the best way to keep me safe and secure at this event is for you to pose as my date," she said, picking up their empty plates to carry them to the sink.

"I don't think that's necessary."

"Have you ever attended a charity gala? Several hundred people, dim lights, entertainment. It's a crush of one or two do-gooders and D.C.'s wealthiest hoping to see and be seen."

"Are you trying to talk me out of agreeing to you attending this event?"

"No, I'm just saying if you're next to me, then I'll be safe, and you can get eyes on any suspicious characters."

He knew she was right and had considered proposing the same idea, but he didn't think it would be believable for her to show up with someone like him.

"You can easily play the part of a handsome bachelor from out of town. No one needs to know you're a dedicated police officer on the job. We can make up our narrative." She looked vulnerable as she stood fiddling with a napkin at the counter.

"Okay, if it'll make you feel safer. What's the dress code? Do I need to grab my penguin suit, or will a suit do?"

Her eyes flashed with interest. "Oh, penguin suit, for sure. It's a thousand dollars a plate charity event for children."

He tried not to seem shocked by the type of money she and her ilk threw around. The difference in their worlds was lit up with neon already.

"I had a ticket for a date. My sister was supposed to come home, but she decided Italy sounded more fun."

He nodded. "Okay, I'll take a look at the venue online tonight and confirm we can secure it. You should get some sleep."

"Will you be here all night with me? I mean, in my con-do?"

"Until midnight. Jake and I will rotate with a third of-ficer. Two officers at all times, one in the apartment, and one in the garage. We'll do sixteen hours on, eight hours off. I'll be back in the morning."

"Okay, good night."

"Thank you for dinner."

He couldn't hide the fact that he was surprised she was so down to earth and a great cook.

She rewarded him with a big smile before departing the living room. He watched her hips sway as she walked down the hall. This was shaping up to be a challenging assignment, and it was only day one.

Chapter Six

DABBING MORE CONCEALER under her eyes, Ainsley tried to cover up the dark circles a sleepless night created. It should be from worry, but in reality, it was images of Rory that ran through her brain all night. Maybe she would find him less attractive after another few days of his watchful eyes tracking her every move. Since it was Saturday, she didn't need to be in the office at her usual five a.m. and tried to sleep in but gave up when she heard the front door open and close.

Listening at her bedroom door, she heard Rory's voice and wondered if he'd managed to get any sleep. She quickly dressed in fitted black leggings, a sports bra, and a long sleeve t-shirt. Walking out into the hallway, she could smell coffee and found Rory alone in the living room.

"Did you get any rest?"

His eyes moved over her fitness ensemble, and she was surprised to find him dressed casually in jeans and a navy-blue T-shirt. He hadn't shaved, and the beginnings of scruff highlighted his squared jaw and outlined his full lips. He looked rugged and clean-cut at the same time.

"I just got back. There's a coffee for you if you're interested." He nodded toward the kitchen counter.

"Thank you." She recognized the coffee company's nautical logo. "This is my favorite. What else does my police file say about me?"

His deep laugh warmed her before she could sip the coffee.

"There's no file. Sailor's has the best coffee in town and they like cops, so it's my go-to."

"Still, it's interesting we go to the same coffee shop but have never run into each other there. I would remember seeing you."

She couldn't help but wonder if fate would have put them in each other's path at some point and then shook the romantic notion away.

"Were you planning to get in a workout?" he asked as his eyes ran over her figure again. He didn't challenge why she found him so memorable. Maybe he wasn't interested in flirting with her after all.

"Yoga. I usually try to make it to a few classes each week."

His brow furrowed.

"By the look on your face, I'm guessing I'll have to settle for a workout in my building's gym?"

Taking a deep breath, he ran a hand absently through his lush locks. His light brown hair was short on the sides but with more length in the subtle waves on top to be mussed.

"I think we could make it work if you're willing to try a different yoga studio. Somewhere out of your usual pattern."

"We? As in, you'll do the class with me?"

"Sure, it can't be that hard, and I've already missed a few workouts this week," he said.

Unable to resist laughing, she took another sip of her coffee.

"You'll need to wear something other than jeans."

"I don't live far from here. We can swing by my place and try the yoga spot next to my crossfit gym."

She nodded in shock. Doing yoga with him felt intimate, like a date, but obviously, it wasn't. He was being very accommodating. Did he always work out with protectees?

"Do you wanna grab something to eat first?" he asked.

"No, I usually just do coffee before a morning workout."

"Huh, me too."

He walked toward the door but paused to call someone.

"Hey, Axe. We're going to take Ms. Nash to the yoga studio on King Street, but first I need to grab something from my place."

She couldn't hear what the other officer said and moved back down the hall to grab her yoga bag, adding an extra towel for him. Then she grabbed two bottles of water and found him waiting at the door.

"Ready?" he asked before opening the door.

Once they were in the car, he told her the name of the yoga studio he had in mind, and she pulled up their webpage. They had forty-five minutes until the next class, and she reserved them two spots.

"Tell me about what to expect in this class?" Rory said.

"We'll be doing power yoga, using our body's weight for resistance. The pace usually fatigues most yogis, but we'll see how you do."

"That sounds like a warning."

"Clearly, you're strong, but yoga requires focus, flexibility, and endurance."

"Challenge accepted, but I choose our next workout."

Smiling out the window, she wondered if she could convince him to spend time with her after this assignment. She'd bet there was a long line of women trying to spend time with him.

Ten minutes later, they were pulling into the driveway of a quaint old Victorian house with a modern refinished front porch. She was impressed he owned an older home in the heart of Old Town Alexandria. It was known as a trendy neighborhood for restaurants but also for beautiful architectural homes.

"Does the historical society give you a hard time about maintaining the architecture of this home?"

"I think they were just happy someone bought it and fixed it up. It was basically condemned when I got it, which was why it was affordable. The requirements to maintain the historical integrity were minimized because there had been a fire."

"That sounds like a big project," she said as he pulled his SUV along the side of the home to the back.

He hopped out and came around to open her door. She spotted another SUV stop at the end of his driveway and assumed it must be the officer he'd spoken to earlier. They used the side door, and she was disappointed she didn't get to check out the front of the home more. Butterflies in her stomach tumbled as he opened his home up to her and ushered her inside a mudroom. Next he typed in a few numbers on a security pad, then ushered her inside to a gorgeous gourmet kitchen. Her eyes bounced from cool light fixtures to the geometric backsplash.

"Don't take this the wrong way, but do you cook?"

There were high ceilings with a crisscross of wooden beams and mixture of modern and rustic accents. Doing a one-eighty she took in the rest of the open space. Wood floors the color of her favorite milk chocolate, navy-blue custom cabinets, and a large kitchen island covered in white marble. The space flowed into a large living room.

"My mom helped select kitchen features, but I do cook a little."

"Wow."

Walking beyond the kitchen, she found a spacious living room with big leather couches, a fireplace, and a huge television mounted on the wall. There were large framed prints of a lake along one wall, and a few framed photos on a bookshelf.

Rory stood back as she took in his space, as if he enjoyed seeing her there among his things. She picked up the largest framed photo with what she assumed was his family.

"That's the Maguire clan on my sister's wedding day," he said, moving closer.

They were all dressed to the nines, and Rory had a big smile for the camera.

"Your sister looks very happy. No wonder, from the way her handsome husband is looking at her." She laughed, setting the photo back down and picking up another smaller frame of Rory with two men that looked a lot like him.

"Charlotte deserves to be happy. Caleb is her second husband. She was married to my best friend but was widowed after only a few years of marriage."

Her eyes shot up to meet his. "I'm so sorry. That must have been horrible for both of you."

Clearing his throat, he nodded and pointed to the other photo she held.

"Those are my brothers, Conner and Finn."

"Your poor mother with three gorgeous sons. She was probably chasing girls out of the house when you were all in high school." She could tell he didn't mean to mention the death of his best friend and didn't want to talk about it, so she tried to lighten the mood.

"Our mom is always telling us to settle down and find a woman who can put up with us, but so far, it hasn't worked."

The air in the room suddenly felt warm as she stared into his deep green eyes. He was standing near and she could easily close the space between them, but then what? They just met, he was assigned to protect her, and she was going to what? Put the moves on him? And what moves? She'd never been good at dating. It always felt like a weird game. Trying to guess what someone was after. Were they interested in her or her family connections?

"I'm just going to change. Stay here," Rory said, ending the moment.

His voice was gruff, and he turned abruptly to head up the wide wood stairs near the front door.

She collapsed on the soft leather of his couch, and the cool material felt soothing on her heated skin. Her heart was pounding. Had he felt the same rush of desire? Part of her hoped her father figured out what was going on fast and the other part of her wanted Rory to protect her indefinitely.

A few minutes later, he reappeared in athletic shorts, a black T-shirt, and sneakers. The muscles of his legs made it obvious he worked out a lot, and his shoulders pulled the material of his shirt snug over his back. Her mouth was dry as she pulled herself off the couch. She wished she was into hot yoga where all the men took their shirts off because she would love to see Rory remove his. She caught a glimpse of some kind of scar along his right bicep but was too distracted by his athletic build to focus on it.

"You sure you're up for this?" he said, holding a duffle bag she'd just noticed.

The worry on his face snapped her out of staring at his chest.

She took a few steps away from him. "Yes, I need to exert some energy. We have twenty minutes until class starts, and the website said we need to complete their registration."

He met her at the door, hit a few numbers on his security keypad, and then ushered her back outside and into his car.

Her legs bounced nervously as he drove the few blocks and parked along the street near the yoga studio. Her palms were sweaty, and she hadn't even considered someone at the studio would recognize her until they were checking in. The woman at the front desk whispered to Rory.

"Is your girlfriend on the news?"

Rory smiled and put his finger up to his lips as if it was a secret. "She likes to try to blend in."

"Oh, no problem. We get a lot of D.C. famous in here. You know the first lady's sister even does yoga here sometimes," the young woman said.

Rory feigned being impressed before placing his hand on Ainsley's lower back. A tingle of awareness ran over her skin, pushing goosebumps up over her arms. Before the woman could say anything more, the doors to one of the studios opened up, and people began to flood the foyer. The class before theirs had ended, and they could make their way inside the studio to claim their spots. Rory's grip moved to the side of her waist as the room grew crowded, and he expertly maneuvered them to the other side of the room and into the mostly empty studio.

"I'd prefer we stick to the back of the room, or you can be on the mat in front of me," Rory said, handing her a rolled mat.

"I'll take the corner, and you can be next to me." She avoided his eyes and looked around the large room. The floors were bamboo and murals of yoga symbols adorned the light blue walls. Soft music played as more people joined them in the studio and claimed their spots. Without talking, she showed him how to set up his mat and grabbed a few of the yoga bricks and belts used during some practices to help with more difficult poses. It was clear Rory was in exceptional shape, but she was curious how limber or tense he was.

Sitting on her mat, she went through a few stretches, and his body bent easily, mimicking her moves. A few minutes later, a man in pink yoga pants with no shirt sat at the front of the class. His muscles were on full display for the audience.

"Oh, shit," Rory whispered.

"Do you know him?" she asked.

"No, but I've seen him at my gym before. He must train

people in both places. He's ruthless."

Just then, the instructor spotted them and nodded at Rory.

"This is going to be brutal," Rory said.

She laughed. She was going to enjoy seeing Rory in every pose.

An hour later, Ainsley rolled her head over to find Rory looking back at her as the instructor-led them through the final Savasana—a breathing exercise that left her wanting a nap. He had removed his shirt about twenty minutes into the class, and she'd missed more than one step, enjoying the lines of muscles along his back, and the coils of his forearms that ran up to his large biceps. His thigh muscles had strained during several balance poses, but his athleticism impressed her.

"Your yoga kicked my butt," he whispered.

She smiled as the instructor asked everyone to take a final seated pose. They did as directed, and she was gifted with the sight of Rory's six-pack before finding her seat and closing her eyes. The instructor's deep voice whispered a thank you to the class for being present and working hard.

Then the entire class replied with, "Namaste."

When she opened her eyes again, Rory looked deep in thought as he sat with his legs outstretched in front of him. Before she could say anything, the instructor's large form folded to kneel in front of them.

"Sergeant, nice to see you today. I take it your girl convinced you there was more to working out than just lifting weights?"

"Something like that." Rory smiled, not correcting him.

"Is it always this tough, or did you ratchet it up for me?"

The instructor smiled. "Come back again and find out," he said, and then he was gone.

"How about some breakfast?" Rory asked.

"Okay, but my treat. I'm pretty sure protection doesn't mean paying for everything."

When they arrived for yoga, he had paid before she had a chance to offer. She was sad to see him put his shirt back on but excited to know she had the rest of the day with him.

Instead of getting into his truck, he shot Axe a text, and they walked a few feet to a local diner.

They ordered omelets and French toast to split, and she almost forgot they weren't on a real date. Until she caught another glimpse of the scar on his arm.

"I know I shouldn't ask, and you don't have to tell me, but that looks like a serious injury on your bicep."

He nodded while concentrating on the eggs on his plate.

"Gunshot, it sorta tore up my arm before exiting the meaty part of my bicep. The scar looks worse than it should because it took me too long to get it stitched up."

"Why did it take you so long?"

His eyes looked sad as he gazed over her shoulder as if he was back in the moment he'd been shot.

"The night my best friend was shot and killed, we were outgunned. We were serving a warrant with the Marshal Service. They had a solid lead on a fugitive hanging out at his girlfriend's house. She wanted him gone. The perp was supposed to be home alone, but somehow, they missed the fact that several of his fugitive friends were with him and they had a lot of firepower. Everything went sideways, and

Sam was fatally wounded. I tried to pull him out and got shot in the process. By the time the medics got to him, it was too late for Sam.

"I let them wrap my arm, but I had to see my sister before I could worry about myself. My dad met me at my sister's place, and we told her together. It was the worst thing I've ever had to do. You'd think my sister would hate me after that."

His eyes finally met hers and she could see all the pain and regret swirling there. She couldn't resist reaching out and clutching his hand. She was surprised he'd shared so much with her.

"I'm so sorry you had to go through that. Your job is really dangerous. I'm sure your sister was just grateful Sam didn't die alone, and that you didn't die too."

She ran her fingers along the back of his hand and felt the charge of heat between them. Pulling his hand back, he took a big gulp of his juice.

"Well, Charlotte is a better person than me, but that doesn't absolve me."

"You can't blame yourself for your friend's death."

"No, I blame the thug that shot him five times, but I do blame myself for not protecting Sam. As the leader of the SWAT team that night, I should have been better prepared and challenged the Marshal's intel before we went in guns blazing."

There was no point in arguing with him. He was carrying around a lot of guilt and needed to deal with it on his own terms. They finished eating, and when the waitress arrived with the bill, he handed her some cash before she could dig out her card.

"We better get rolling if I'm going to be glammed up for this event tonight," he said with a forced smile and change of subject.

"Thank you for sharing some of your story with me and going to yoga. I'm looking forward to the gala tonight, even if we're just pretending."

His hand settled on her back, and he didn't let go until she stepped up into his SUV. They were both quiet on the ride back to her place. It was strange how close she felt to a man she'd only met twenty-four hours ago but knew nothing between them was real. His job was to babysit her, and she doubted if he had the choice, he'd go to yoga again. Besides, she needed to focus on what story was brewing on the Hill. She needed to keep her eye on the prize, land a big story, and get the networks to consider her for a correspondent job in New York. Rory was the kind of distraction that could derail a girl's plans.

Chapter Seven

AFTER DROPPING AINSLEY back at her place it was afternoon, and Rory needed to get some space from her. Leaving Axe in charge while she got ready for the gala, he made his excuses and planned to be back by six. It'd been nice getting out of his typical routine and doing something normal with her, but it wasn't real. She was his protectee, an assignment that could end abruptly when her dad decided she didn't need any protection after all.

The odd thing was, he never told anyone about what happened to Sam or his scar. He usually lied and said it was from a broken bone as a kid. It was just easier not to rehash losing his best friend, but for some reason, he'd wanted Ainsley to know what had happened. That he'd failed, and that was the reason he was so strict with protocols. The more attention to detail, the less likely he'd be surprised again.

Instead of heading home to rest, he found himself driving over to his folks' house. Late afternoon on a Saturday meant his mother was probably baking and his dad was fiddling around in the yard. He wanted to talk to one or both of them about the job offer at training. Pulling into the driveway that ran along the side of the house, he spotted his dad working outside on some kind of motion sensor.

"Hey, old man. You need some help?"

His dad's eyes squinted. "Who you calling old?" But his green eyes brightened with a smile as he stood and gave Rory a big hug.

No matter how old he and his siblings got, they were never too old for a hug from either of their parents.

"What are you up to today?" his dad asked as he squatted back down and fiddled with the angle of what looked like a motion light.

"I got this new security system for the lawn with these megawatt motion sensor lights, but your mom said it's too bright. Every time a bunny hops in our yard, it lights up the master bedroom, so I'm looking for another angle."

Rory shook his head, knowing he didn't want any part of his dad's grand scheme to turn his childhood home into Fort Knox.

"What do you need this system for? If Finn is here, you got your own commando sleeping down the hall every night."

"Your brother is here and there, but he shouldn't have to worry about taking down some intruder. He needs to rest."

"Dad, you have a security system on the house and live in the suburbs. Is there something I need to know about?"

"Your mother says I'm paranoid, and maybe I am. But why not have as many deterrents as we can? You know, proper lighting is one of the top five deterrents for a break-in." His dad started to rattle off his home security stats.

"I know, I know. Why don't we get you a dog since it's the number one deterrent? Then the dog would keep you busy. Two problems solved."

"I'm still trying to convince your mother. She's worried a puppy will pee all over her nice rugs."

"I'm sure she's right." He laughed.

"So what'd you want to talk about?" his dad said.

The air was still cool, but the crisp weather of the morning had burned off with the afternoon sun. It was that iffy time of year when spring was trying to roll in but not quite warm enough to be outside for long periods.

"Come on, I'll make you some coffee while you tell me what's bugging you."

Following his dad into the house, he could smell the freshly baked muffins before he spotted them on the kitchen counter, but there was no sign of his mom.

"Your mother went out to lunch with her book club, but she made sure to leave us something." His dad fiddled with the coffeemaker as Rory took a seat on a stool at the large island and grabbed a muffin.

"Captain Sullivan offered me a job as director of training."

His dad nodded and brought over two cups of coffee. "That's a big job, a good job too. Are you ready for a new challenge?"

He tried to decipher his father's neutral expression. Ever since he was a kid, his folks avoided telling him and his siblings what decisions to make. They offered advice and any experience that might pertain to the issue but never pushed any of them to go one way or the other. Free will, his dad would always say. You have to make up your mind on what feels important, what feels right.

"I don't know. I've been content on the SWAT team,

but it has been eight years. Maybe I do need to try something different."

"Whelp, it's a prestigious job, so your management believes in you and your ability to do it. But you know it'll feel a lot like walking away from the streets, and then it may feel daunting to get back to them later. That said, I think there comes a time when every officer should take a step back and switch things up drastically. Training would be very rewarding and probably frustrating at the same time."

"Like my current assignment, I'm pulling protection for a senator's daughter."

His dad sipped his coffee and nodded his head as if he already knew. "Your brother Conner mentioned that."

"How he knows everything that goes on in this city is a mystery to me."

They both laughed. "Connie was always wanting to know everything about everyone. Even when you were all kids, he always knew what everyone was up to."

"Maybe I should ask him what I should do since he probably already knows what it is," Rory said, earning another laugh from his old man.

"How is Finn doing?" Rory asked.

"He's alright. Been quiet since he got home. You know, he won't talk about what made him ready to leave the team, other than the pace of ops was grueling. I think he's processing it and keeping himself busy with law school."

"Mom must be ecstatic one of her kids followed in her footsteps, finally."

"She is. You know, Finn will always be her baby, even if he was a Navy SEAL. Tell me about this girl you're protecting? Is she as glamorous as the TV makes her out to be? Is she cooperating?"

"The kind of woman who knows what she wants for sure. She and her father have a strained relationship, but I get the feeling the senator is truly worried about her safety. She's all about chasing the next big story. I guess to make a splash in her career."

"And? Is she single?"

Rory stood and set his now-empty cup in the sink. "Yes, she's single and a rolling stone."

"Last I checked, you were still single. I'm just saying, don't rule her out because she's on TV or the daughter of a politician."

"I don't think she'd be interested in dating someone with my lifestyle."

"So maybe there is another point for the new job. You could work normal hours and focus more on your personal life. You know Charlotte can't be expected to be the only one giving us grandkids," his dad said.

"I think that is my cue to get outta here. Thanks for the coffee and the advice."

His dad gave him another hug and walked him outside.

"We'll see you tomorrow for family dinner. No excuses. And bring your lady friend with you."

"She's not mine, Dad," Rory called as he walked back to his SUV.

"We'll see," his dad hollered back.

Driving away, an image of Ainsley popped up in his mind. He barely knew her, but he was looking forward to spending more time with her, even if it was for work. Maybe he had been on the SWAT team for too long. He forgot what it was like to spend time with someone and get to know them on a personal level. He didn't think for a second that Ainsley would be interested in spending time with him after this assignment, but she did seem to be making the best of it so far. She asked him to act as her date instead of her body-guard, and he was going to play the part. Why not enjoy an evening out with a beautiful woman?

Chapter Eight

A INSLEY SPENT THE last hour in her room getting ready and was excited to see Rory dressed up. At the same time, nervous flutters settled in her belly at the idea of pretending he was her date. The man was hot, with a type of power she wasn't accustomed to being around. Rich men that came from affluent families always had an air of self-importance, but it wasn't anything like Rory's raw manly confidence.

A knock on her door broke through her thoughts.

"Ms. Nash, a car service arrived, but we're going to have Jake act as our driver tonight," Rory called through her closed door.

He'd said a few other officers would join them at the gala to provide additional coverage, since the event was so large.

Taking one last look at her figure draped in a cobalt blue gown with a boat neck and cuffs on her shoulders, she was glad she didn't overdo it on the French toast that morning. The dress was fitted, and the velvet material showed every curve. Enjoying the feel of a plush rug under her feet, she padded over to the door and opened it to find Rory looking down into his phone.

"Will Jake moonlight as a chauffeur all night, or are you

going to let him join us at the party?" she asked.

She waited for a beat until he lifted his head and watched as his eyes scanned over her body before meeting her eyes. Her skin warmed under his scrutiny, and she hoped he liked what he saw. She smiled when he stayed mute but held her breath when he took a deep inhale.

"You look…" He paused.

"Nice? Sexy? Glamorous? Like I'm trying too hard?"

She let her own gaze run up and down his insanely built form wrapped in a tuxedo and wondered how enjoyable it must have been for the tailor to take his measurements. She would thoroughly enjoy the chance to run her hands along his long legs, tapered waist, hard abs, and thick muscular chest up over his large shoulders. His sexy smolder stole her breath as their eyes locked.

"It's not appropriate for me to say how beautiful you look, but it feels awkward not stating the obvious."

She caught the glimpse of the dimple in his left cheek before his eyes skirted over her mouth. If she were any good at reading minds, she would swear he wanted to say more.

"Thank you for not giving me a compliment, Sergeant. I know we don't want this situation to get any more awkward, but you look fantastic in a tux."

Her hands itched to smooth his lapels as she wondered if his muscles would pop out the back. He looked accustomed to the supple material that swayed with his movements. An underlying confidence he carried in his uniform was just as enticing, with his ripped physique wrapped in the black tux and crisp white shirt. The black onyx buttons led down his chest like clues to a treasure.

"Do all SWAT members have standard issued formal menswear hanging in their lockers, in case the need arises?"

She enjoyed teasing him because he seemed so reserved and in control. Exactly how a person would want their assigned protective officer to be. Before he could answer, she turned back into her room, leaving the door open for him. Plucking a pair of earrings from a jewelry box she kept in the top drawer of her dresser, she waited to see if Rory would follow her.

He hovered at the doorway.

"This getup is left over from my man-of-honor duty at my sister's wedding."

"Your sister has exceptional taste."

He smiled and nodded but didn't add any additional information.

"Jake will drive us, and then he and two more teammates will act as event security. It's not too late for me to hang back as your hired bodyguard for the night."

Putting the stud diamonds in each ear, she noted the tension in his voice and smiled. Sitting on the bench in front of her bed, she leaned forward to fix the clasp on her silver stilettos before meeting his eyes. With his features schooled he studied her, but she had no idea what he was thinking.

"We agreed it begs too many questions if I show up with a bodyguard and could tip off anyone who is possibly watching my routine. If you attend the event as my plus one, no one will know I have a police protective detail."

Standing, she walked closer to where he stood against the doorway of her room. He didn't back up, and she stopped an inch away. Reaching up, she grasped his bow tie in her hands and pretended to straighten it as an excuse to touch him.

"Do you think you can manage to pretend to be my date? You'll need to feign romantic interest in me." She smoothed her hands down the folds of his lapel, meeting his gaze.

Being this close to him, his crisp clean scent wafted around her, and his body heat made her want to get closer.

"I doubt that would be challenging for any man," he said with a steady voice.

Staring up in his evergreen eyes, her heart was pounding and her skin pebbled from the heat of desire as it coursed through her. There was no denying Rory Maguire was a gorgeous, no-nonsense man, but she wanted to see him with his guard down.

"You're going to cause a stir at this event, but that can't be helped," she said, taking a step back, but his warm, rough hand caught her bicep and he leaned forward. His breath was on her neck, and his freshly shaved jaw rubbed her cheek ever so slightly.

"I'll try not to embarrass you with my neanderthal ways," he said into her ear. "I'm quite good at using a fork instead of my hands when I eat."

He pulled away, and a smirk spread across his face, pushing his dimple into his cheek deeper than she realized it could plunge.

He was taunting her with his sex appeal, proving he recognized the attraction between them.

A giddy laugh bubbled up even as her knees wobbled from his touch.

"I'll try not to enjoy having you so close to me tonight,

since we're only playing a role. But I'll warn you, when other women start to hit on you, I'm not going to just let them disrespect me. Even if you're only my pretend date."

"Likewise, Ms. Nash," he said before letting go of her arm.

Taking a deep breath, she wondered how far she should push her luck with him. He was unbelievably sexy before he put on the tux. Now he was irresistible. There were at least a dozen naughty things she'd do to him before they made it to the event, if he really were her date. How was she going to focus on the speech she was due to give with him by her side?

"You better start calling me Ainsley, or everyone will think I paid you to be my date."

"Don't worry, Ainsley. No one will question my interest in you tonight."

✕

FLASHING LIGHTS, A red carpet, and Rory was already the belle of the ball. Women were practically swooning before they could even make it through the foyer of the Shakespeare Library where the charity event was being held in downtown D.C.. She had taken up a stance to greet people along with the charity representative, but everyone was flocking to Rory. She couldn't blame them as he stood next to her with such a commanding presence.

"Let's make our way inside," she suggested, not wanting the charity representative to feel slighted.

The library had gone under a huge renovation, and this was her first visit to the new great hall that served as a posh venue for exhibits and events. Walking through the gold-encrusted doors, Ainsley gripped Rory's bicep as he scanned the elegant room. The venue had thirty-foot ceilings, crystal chandeliers dimmed for ambiance, and stained-glass windows of modern works of art back lit, sending cascades of color over the crowded space. There were wall-to-wall D.C. elites dressed up to impress.

"This room is as big as a football field, so no wandering off," Rory said.

"Oh, don't worry. I'm happy to be the clingy girlfriend tonight." She moved her body closer and slid her hand into his, weaving their fingers together.

He'd been looking everywhere but at her until now.

"Marking your territory?"

She smiled at his sudden display of humor. "Yes."

His eyes narrowed, and he pursed his lips before looking away.

"There's Tate." He nodded toward the bar on their left where a black man in a fitted tux with a white dinner jacket stared at them. "And Axe is the guy near the makeshift stage," Rory said.

Axe had white-blonde hair, a trimmed beard, and also looked like Rambo in his tux; she was convinced he used a bandana for a pocket square.

"Is it a requirement to be hot and ripped to get on the SWAT team?"

Rory coughed. "Yes, whenever we have a new team member, we always have glamour shots taken before we let them graduate from the ten weeks of grueling training. Just to make sure they won't embarrass us."

"His name is Axe?" she asked, ignoring his sarcasm.

"Axel Ross is his full name. His dad was a die-hard Guns N' Roses fan, but it suits him. Trust me."

"I'll take your word for it. Can you please stop getting so much attention? I'm not used to feeling so possessive, and I need to concentrate on my speech." She nudged him toward the line leading to the bar on the side of the room where Jake stood watching the crowd.

He leaned down to whisper into her ear, and his warm breath sent a shiver down to her toes.

"Did I do something wrong?" he asked.

She took advantage of his nearness and stepped closer to him, pretending to fiddle with his buttons.

"If you mean having every woman checking you out, then yes, you did." She pulled him closer and stood up on her tiptoes to whisper in his ear. "It won't kill you to at least appear interested in me instead of looking everywhere else."

His scruff tickled her cheek, and she breathed in his scent—no cologne, just soap and man. Before he could respond, she pulled away, not wanting to make him too uncomfortable or fall for her own tricks.

When he pulled her back into him and his hand snaked up her neck, her chest fluttered with warmth and something new. His thumb stroked her chin, and he didn't speak until had her full attention.

"Truthfully, I would prefer to be here only as your date, but unfortunately, I'm working. That means keeping an eye out for anyone suspicious to keep you safe."

She was captivated by the intensity in his now dark eyes and watched as he licked his lower lip. She shifted her cheek into his hand, unable to control the instinctive need to be closer to him. But he dropped his palm while his other arm gently pressed her lower back, encouraging her to move forward in the line.

The urge to kiss him was startling, but that was not part of the agreed plan tonight. He was her date so he could stay close to her in the crowded gala, raising money for her favorite charity. She needed to focus and work the room to raise as much money as possible.

"What are you drinking?" he asked.

"What?" She looked around and realized they were holding up the line at the bar. "Champagne please."

Rory ordered her bubbly drink and a soda water before slipping the bartender a tip and then guiding her away from the line.

"I need to socialize a little before the speeches, and then we can enjoy the event a bit."

Rory nodded and dutifully followed as she said hello to several longtime donors for the event. She introduced him as her date, and each person commented on what an attractive couple they were or how impressive Rory's broad shoulders were. A half-hour later, the lights were flickering to indicate the sit-down portion of the evening would begin soon.

"We need to find your table," he said, looping his arm around her waist and letting his hand settle on her hip.

The crowd of people began to move toward the other end of the room, where the tables were set.

She smiled up at him, itching to kiss the stubble on his chin, but resisted. Instead, she followed his lead as he began to move through the crowd. Several women stared openly as they passed by. She held her head high and enjoyed the admiration, as if she'd won a prize by having Rory as her date. No one needed to know they were pretending. The crowd swelled just beyond the dance floor as guests searched for their tables, and he pulled her even closer into his side.

Another heated glance from him, and she couldn't help but wonder if they'd both stopped playing a role the moment they stepped inside the venue.

"Ainsley, for some reason I didn't expect to see you tonight," said an accusatory tone to her left.

The sound of a pompous New England accent caused her to flinch. Rory slowed his pace, having heard the man too, and looked down at her with a subtle, inquisitive expression. She plastered on a smile and turned, placing her back against Rory's chest.

"Good evening, George. I'm not sure why you thought I wouldn't attend tonight, considering I am the keynote speaker and on the board for this charity."

George forced a fake smile and looked beyond her to Rory.

"What's this? Did you hire an escort in some pathetic attempt to convince people you've already moved on?"

"Wow, George. Be careful. Your jealous streak is on full display. I might actually think you still had feelings for me if I didn't already know your feelings were only geared toward my father and a political career."

Before she could say anything else, Rory stuck out his hand toward her ex-boyfriend. "Rory Maguire. It's a pleasure to meet the fool that let this stunning woman slip through his hands."

George scoffed before turning his back and walking away.

She laughed. "That was well said."

"Guys like that never have much to say when faced with men who represent everything they lack."

"How could you know all of that after meeting him for two seconds and it took me months?"

He just winked before pulling her by the hand to keep moving beyond the crowd.

After finding their table, she gladly stayed put while the lights began to flicker again. Rory unbuttoned his tux jacket and draped one arm around the back of her chair as he scanned the crowd. His body heat warmed her, and his thumb ran up and down her shoulder in a torturous lazy circle. His coworker Axe nodded at them, and she couldn't help but lean into Rory's warmth.

"Notice anyone out of place yet?" she asked.

"Besides me?"

"You fit in fine. But be careful while I'm on stage."

A young woman she'd met in the lead-up to planning the event approached with a mic attached to a headband and a clipboard.

"Ms. Nash, if you'll follow me to the stage, we can get the event started once everyone has settled in. Then we'll have a light meal followed by the casino night."

"Great, showtime." She took another sip of her champagne before arching up to kiss Rory's cheek. His skin was warm on her lips, and she wished she were brave enough to kiss his mouth. "Good luck fending off your admirers."

Rory cleared his throat as his hand gripped her chin,

forcing her to face his stormy eyes. "Be careful and stay low if anything crazy happens. I'll get to you."

"I'm not worried about that at all. Just be ready to ramp up your interest in me once my speech is over, or your fan club will eat you alive."

With a sideways glance at several women openly staring at them, she placed a featherlight kiss on his lips. But once she'd created the moment, he held her chin in place, returning the kiss for several beats longer than a casual peck before ending it.

"I have a feeling you might be the dangerous one in this room," he said, clearing his throat.

"Ditto," she said before standing up on legs that felt like mush and heading to the stage.

Chapter Nine

THREE HOURS LATER, he exhaled the tension he'd felt all night, battling himself to keep his eyes on the room and not Ainsley's figure. They were back in the SUV and could drop their faux routine of an affectionate couple, but Ainsley still reached for his hand. Looking at her in the dimly lit back seat, she smiled with a telltale glaze in her eyes from the champagne. He reminded himself for probably the one-hundredth time that this was all a mirage and he needed to remain professional.

"Did you all find anyone suspicious tonight?" she asked.

"Tell me more about your ex. How motivated is he for a political career?" he asked, hoping to distract Jake from noticing how clingy she was.

Ainsley groaned. "George Constantine Kennedy, no relation to the Kennedys. He's a lawyer and aspires to win the expected vacant senate seat next year in New York."

"Why did he say he was surprised to see you at your event tonight?" Rory held her hand firmly when she made a move to pull it away.

"We had a public breakup orchestrated by his other girlfriend a few weeks ago."

"Other girlfriend?"

"George decided to invest his time in two political families, increasing his odds that one would pan out. Natalie Spencer's father is a congressman from Maine."

"Majority leader of the House, that's a big name to aspire to," Jake commented.

"Your political acumen is sharp, Jake. I'm sure my father would welcome you on his team if you're looking for a change of scenery," Ainsley said.

"Oh, I think the scoundrels on the Hill are more vicious than the criminals we deal with, but I like to know who is making decisions for the country," Jake said.

"So you think your ex's only goal was to align himself with a powerful political family, but he wouldn't be violent?"

"I guess you never know, but he didn't flinch when I ended it. He already had a plan B. I have no desire whatsoever to be part of some fake politically motivated marriage."

"Sounds like you dodged a bullet." Rory squeezed her hand before letting go.

Jake pulled into the garage, placing them right at the entrance.

"Sit tight, please," he said before she could reach for her door. "I'll come around to get your door."

Ainsley nodded.

"Same as last night, Axe can relieve you at midnight." Rory patted Jake's shoulder, who nodded while staring ahead to look for any anomalies.

Exiting the backseat of the SUV, he scanned the dark garage. His hand instinctively patted his pistol hanging from his shoulder harness, hidden under his tux.

Spotting a shadow that looked out of place near the garage entrance, he moved forward of the car, keeping a cement beam between him and the shadow. Still in the driver's seat, Jake flipped his brights on at the garage entrance, and the shadow turned into a figure in all black that sprinted out toward the water. Rory pushed off into a sprint and gritted his teeth at the lack of traction on his dress shoes. The cold air was moist along the water as he followed the sounds of feet pounding the sidewalk.

"Stop," he shouted, but the figure continued down the wide sidewalk where runners followed the path through various routes along the river. Knowing it was unlikely he would catch the man, he worried if more than one person was waiting for them in the garage and stopped in his tracks. Turning around, he ran faster back to Ainsley's building.

By the time he made it, Axe had arrived and was out searching the garage.

"It's clear, man. That guy musta been on foot to get here."

"Damn it," Rory said, breathing heavily from his sprint. "Sit tight while I check the lobby." He called out to Axe and held his hand up to Jake, signaling all was not clear.

They were all trained in silent hand signals to communicate during various tactical incidents when voice communication wasn't possible.

Moving into the lobby, he hugged the marble wall and listened. There was the sound of a radio and soft breathing. Could Stanley have drifted off to sleep? Not a great sign from a security perspective.

"I know you're there, Sergeant," Stanley called out.

Unable to fight the smile, Rory peeked around the corner, leading with his gun. "Any trouble tonight, Stanley?"

"No, not until you pulled up. Then it felt like I was watching a James Bond movie on the garage security screen. Don't know how I didn't see that guy lurking."

"He was in all black and stuck to the shadows. I only caught a glimpse," Rory said, offering the doorman some sympathy. After all, he wasn't a security guard.

Rory looked around the back of the desk where Stanley sat to ensure the old man wasn't being forced to say everything was fine.

"Nothing to see here, Sarg," Stanley said, holding his hands up.

"Anyone come around this evening that you didn't recognize?"

"No."

"Any deliveries? Any cars that didn't belong?"

"No, and no."

"Alright, I'm going to clear the condo before I bring Ms. Nash up. Stay alert."

"Yes, sir."

Ten minutes later, Rory made his way back down to the garage. He stopped to speak with Axe and let him know the plan. "I'm going to need you to stick around until a patrol officer can relieve you."

"You got it, Sarg. Are we staying low profile, or should I start jacking up visitors?"

"Let's keep it as low as possible, but if anyone is buzzing up, ask for ID and run their names."

"Done." Axe rubbed his hands together as if he were looking forward to a visitor.

Rory opened Ainsley's door and was hit with a wave of concern. Her face was pale, and she was clinching a tissue.

"Are you okay?" he asked in a low tone.

"No. Who was that in the garage? What took you so long upstairs, and how were we supposed to know if you were being attacked? Why did you go up alone?" she shouted through gritted teeth.

Rory looked from her anger to Jake, who shrugged. "I explained you had things under control, but she wasn't convinced."

"He wouldn't let me out of the car," she said, pushing her way past Rory.

He stood for a split second, stunned by her reaction, but caught up to her before she could get beyond the door.

"Good luck in the doghouse," Jake hollered out from the car where he'd left the door open.

"Ainsley, slow down. I go first. Remember?"

"That was before you acted so reckless, and besides, you already cleared the foyer."

She followed him into the hallway and tried to stalk past him, but he stopped her by gripping her elbows.

"But someone could be lying in wait. You never know," he said.

Ainsley stopped in her tracks just inside and spun to face him. "Like I'm being hunted, and someone will find a way to get to me? As in, not even you and all your training and muscles or guns can keep me safe?"

Rory enveloped her in his arms. "No, you're safe with me. But I like to plan for the unexpected. I like to assume someone will try to outsmart me, and I'll be ready for them."

Ainsley stood with her arms at her sides, unwilling to embrace him back, but resting her head on his chest.

"I can understand how unsettling it must have been to see someone lurking in the garage and me sprinting after them." He rubbed her back in an attempt to soothe her as a weight settled in his gut. Whoever was lurking in the garage was causing Ainsley to cry, and it was pissing him off. Meanwhile, he shouldn't be feeling anything because she was a work assignment.

She took a deep breath and slid her hands under his jacket to hug his waist tightly.

"I'm sorry," he said, unsure exactly what he was apologizing for, but he didn't want her to be so upset. He let his chin rest on her head as she took a few more deep breaths.

"You're fast, even in dress shoes," she said, still hugging him tightly.

"Not fast enough tonight."

"Will he come back?"

"I don't know, but he'll regret it if he does."

"I want to get out of this dress," she said, pulling back and looking up at him.

Swallowing the lump in his suddenly dry throat, he clenched his teeth.

"That I can't help you with, but we should get you to bed."

He flinched at the implication, then took her hands from around his waist. Unwilling to break all contact, he held one of her hands as he led her down the hall.

"Ms. Nash, don't you fret. We have D.C.'s finest to secure the building."

"Thank you, Stanley. You should be careful too," she said as they passed him standing at attention.

She was quiet in the elevator, still clutching his hand, and followed his lead. Once inside her condo, she slipped off her shoes and carried them back to her room.

Rory watched as she walked down the hall, not trying to be glamorous and alluring but unable to help it. He could see her door was open after he poured them each a glass of water but waited in the living room to see if she would seek him out to talk more. Shucking his jacket, bowtie, and cufflinks, he felt more comfortable, yet a tinge of worry lingered. Before tonight, it was only a possibility Ainsley was in danger. Now he thought there may be a real need for him.

"Rory, can you please sit with me until I fall asleep?"

Looking up, she stood in the hall in pajama pants and an oversized sweatshirt. Her makeup was gone, and she looked vulnerable and scared but still sexy as hell. After tonight and all the unprofessional thoughts he had about Ainsley, he was officially the worst bodyguard since Kevin Costner.

"Of course." He stood to follow her.

Grabbing the water he poured for her on the way, he hoped he could get some sleep too. There was no point in trekking home when his mind would just be swirling with thoughts of her. At least in her place, he had a better chance to rest knowing two other teammates were on duty. She already had a chair set parallel to the bed only inches away from where she would be laying. Without a word, she climbed in under the covers but sat up, waiting for him to sit. Handing her the water, he sat in the comfortable padded swivel chair.

"Drink," he said.

She took a long sip, then set the glass down and tapped the lamppost to turn it off before laying on her pillow facing him. The only light was from the moon falling through a crack in the curtains and an alarm clock on the opposite side of her bed. He could make out her face as his eyes adjusted and found her looking at him. She reached for his hand resting on the arm of the chair.

"I couldn't sleep last night, and I wasn't even scared yet," she whispered.

Rory squeezed her hand. "Don't be scared. I won't let anyone get near you. Get some sleep."

"If you need to rest, you can lay next to me. I won't ravage you tonight," she said.

He cracked a smile and squeezed her hand but stayed in his chair. Even in exhaustion, she had a sense of humor. It was more than tempting to lay next to her, but that was definitely not an option. Her safety and his job would be on the line if he let his attraction to her get the better of him.

"Good night," he said as her eyes closed.

Stroking the back of her hand with his thumb, he tried to calm his own racing heart. Seeing the figure in the garage had been like a bucket of ice-cold water on his emotions that had been running hot all night. Ainsley was the type of sexy beauty that everyone could acknowledge, but her playful wit was what surprised him. She was equally as smart as she was ambitious, and if he had to guess, she was plotting to climb to the top of her field. He wondered what was driving her, what she was after in life? Not that it should matter to him, since they wouldn't likely see each other after this assignment.

For now, he just needed to concentrate on keeping her safe, and the best way to do that was to start digging around into what the senator and his staff were trying to keep secret. He didn't have any loyalty to the politicians, but he also didn't have any investigative resources. SWAT assignments were reactive to a crime in progress most times. But he had one contact who always seemed to know what was going on in this city—his brother Conner.

Ainsley's breath hitched as her body rolled closer to him, pulling his hand under her cheek. When he tried to pull it back, she clamped down harder, and he had to admit he liked the feel of her skin on his. He'd have to wait a bit and let her get into a deeper sleep before detangling himself from her.

It wouldn't be a hardship at all for him to enjoy her wrapped in his arms, but that was definitely not part of the assignment.

Chapter Ten

T HE SMELL OF bacon woke Ainsley, but before she opened her eyes, she knew she was alone in her room. Rory's presence was distinct, and her hand was empty. She wondered if every protectee received his comforting bedside manner or if she was somehow special. Opening her eyes confirmed she was alone, and the sun was shining high. She padded into the bathroom to brush her teeth before seeing who was talking out in her living room. Five minutes later, the unexpected sight of Rory, Jake, and Axe in her kitchen greeted her.

"Ah, good morning, Ms. Nash. I took the liberty of making you breakfast," Axe said with a smooth country twang. He had deep brown eyes framed by long blond lashes most women would pay a lot of money for, blond hair cut short, dark skin, and full lips spread in a wide smile surrounded by his beard. She bet he used all of his God-given talents to his advantage on more than one occasion.

"Good morning. Axe, right? Nice to officially meet you," Ainsley said, moving to sit in the open seat next to Jake at the counter.

"We were just reviewing some logistics for security," Rory explained.

There was an edge to his voice that was less intimate than he sounded when they spoke alone.

"If you're all up here, then who is downstairs?" she asked.

"My replacement is downstairs, but I couldn't pass up breakfast before I go home to crash," Jake said before shoving a huge bite of pancakes covered in syrup and strawberries in his mouth.

Axe set a heaping plate of food down in front of her and winked when she looked up at him. He'd cut the strawberry into the shape of a tulip bud.

"This must work very well for you with the ladies." She couldn't resist teasing him.

"Oh, I don't know, Ms. Nash. Is it working?"

"Axe," Rory warned.

Ainsley chuckled as she poured syrup over her tower of pancakes and reached for the whipped cream canister. She sprayed three dollops on top of her stack of pancakes, earning a grin from Jake and Axe.

Rory watched with a furrowed brow.

"This is going to be amazing," she said before taking a huge bite.

"Axe is our chef, and he breaks down the doors on raids," Jake explained.

The fluffy cake-like texture of the pancake topped with the whipped cream and bits of strawberry instantly cheered her up. She ate several bites and a piece of bacon before she looked up from her plate.

"This is delicious. I've never had pancakes at home before."

"Sacrilege. I make them every weekend," Axe said.

"That's because you have the appetite of a six-year-old," Jake said.

She couldn't stop smiling and guessed that was part of the plan in providing her with such an amazing breakfast, and she felt grateful. Rory was the only one who seemed grumpy this morning. She suspected he'd slept in the chair in her room all night which probably accounted for his mood.

"Any updates since last night?" she asked, almost worried to find out.

"We've been directed to maintain coverage while the feds investigate," Jake replied.

Rory stopped typing, and his shoulders stiffened. He was probably ready to unload her protection assignment after last night. For some reason, she thought he'd enjoyed playing her date at the gala, and he'd seemed so caring when she asked him to hold her hand as she fell asleep. But now, he was back to all business and seemed annoyed.

"Can we do our own investigation? Maybe see if the junior senator's wife wants to talk?"

Three sets of eyes landed on her.

"I mean, I wouldn't second guess a federal investigation, but I am a journalist and you all are cops. You have to admit there are like a dozen questions rolling around in your minds." She took another glorious bite of the pancakes.

"We haven't been assigned a case to investigate, just your protection," Rory said. "But I can't tell you not to do your job."

Looking up, she swore he was fighting a smirk, and her cheeks ached from the smile it put on her face. He wasn't annoyed with her, just the situation, and she couldn't blame him. She almost forgot Axe and Jake were there until they both coughed.

"You sure you want to risk pissing off your dad?" Rory warned.

"I can handle my dad. It's Jenkins we need to worry about. He's always been more power hungry than any politician I've ever met."

"Maybe he's the one you need to be looking into," Rory said.

"Maybe. Does that mean you're up for doing some snooping around?" she asked.

"No, I'm just here to make sure you don't get hurt. But I doubt your dad expected you to just sit back and wait for the story to be reported by someone else."

"Then eat up because we're going to have a busy day," Ainsley said.

Axe set the rest of the pancakes in front of Rory.

"Alright then, I'm off for a nap. Call me if they get into trouble," Jake said to Axe.

After cleaning her plate, Ainsley helped Axe tidy the kitchen while formulating a plan. She wanted to speak to the wives or girlfriends of anyone close to her dad's protégé, Senator Carter. The women linked to political men always knew far more than anyone expected and usually wanted to talk.

"I'm just going to make a few calls, and then I think we should head to the Potomac Tennis Club. I'd bet there will be a gaggle of political wives there gossiping, and I want to be included," Ainsley said to Rory.

He was sitting in her living room, looking at something on his computer that appeared to be a police report.

"I guess I'll be reprising my role as your boyfriend today?"

"It's the most believable story for why you'd be willing to stick to me like glue all weekend. But don't underestimate this crowd's desire to find a crack in our story."

"Don't worry. I can be as convincing as you need me to be," Rory said low enough for only her to hear.

She wasn't sure if he was teasing her but found his flirty green eyes twinkling. Axe was still fiddling in the kitchen, so she didn't feel comfortable asking him what that might involve. But if she had to guess, he meant he was as attracted to her as she was to him.

An hour later, she was dressed in pink linen pants and a white blouse, and they'd stopped by his place so he could change. Fighting every impulse to snoop, instead, she called the club to book a table for brunch. She only had access because her father had a membership. But she had to admit, the doors opened from her father's career in business and politics gave her unique access to information and people. If she wasn't so mad at her dad, she'd almost be tempted to thank him. Not only had he thought to protect her, but he assigned Rory to her. Which reminded her that she wasn't the only one who could be in danger.

"Do you think my dad is in danger?" she called up the stairs to where Rory had disappeared to change.

His head popped out of a doorway, and she noted his lack of a shirt.

"Hang on, I'll be right down."

She started pacing the herringbone wood floor he had in his foyer and worried if she should reach out to her dad.

Looking up, she spotted Rory looking edible in crisp chino shorts and pulling on a navy-blue polo. He opened a hidden closet by the front door and fished out a pair of boat shoes.

"Is this acceptable for the tennis club?" he asked.

"Yes, you look..." She paused before finishing her thought and gulped.

"What? You won't hurt my feelings, and I'd rather know if I'm going to embarrass myself. Are all the men going to be in those cheesy seersucker suits or something?"

She pictured his ripped physique in a baby-blue-and-white-checkered seersucker and grinned bigger.

"No, not every man, but I'm sure we'll see a few. I was just going to say you look relaxed and gorgeous. I just hope your good looks won't distract the women too much from answering my questions."

Rory stopped in his tracks and squinted his eyes at her. "You should save your act for the club."

Taking two steps forward, she invaded his personal space slowly, pretending to remove a piece of lint from his shirt before smoothing his polo over his muscular chest so she could touch him.

"I'm not pretending to be attracted to you." She lifted her chin up to look him in the eyes and forced herself to own her feelings.

"You know, sometimes in tense situations, people confuse emotions of gratitude for attraction. There are dozens of clinical studies on the subject."

Before he could continue, she stepped up on her tiptoes and kissed him. His lips were firm and soft at the same time. Her hands slid over his shoulders to weave into the hair at the nape of his neck, where his short hair tickled her fingers. He made a moan of pleasure mixed with what sounded like regret as his mouth opened and he deepened the kiss. But his hands didn't pull her closer. He was trying to resist the attraction between them while his mouth told her how much he wanted it too. His tongue stroked hers before his teeth teased her lower lip. Finally, his hands stroked over her forearms right before he gently pulled her hands from his neck, and he took a step back. Without letting go of her, he created distance between them as they both panted to catch their breath.

"I can't, Ainsley. I'll be too distracted to protect you, and I can't risk it."

She nodded, embarrassed by her bold display of desire.

"At least we'll look like a new couple fueled by sexual tension at the club today. Maybe it will keep any of the bored housewives at bay," she said.

"Why do I feel like I'm going to be the vulnerable one today?"

"Don't worry, I'll protect you."

✕

AS EXPECTED, THERE were a dozen politicians' wives having brunch when they entered the club's posh dining room. Another dozen socialites and D.C.'s who's who rounded out the crowd. There was a more casual outdoor space where the people who had come off the courts could lounge over lunch or drinks. Ainsley spotted the group of women she wanted to try to chat with at the edge of the outdoor patio. She asked the hostess to seat them at a table next to theirs.

"After we're seated for a bit, maybe you could go for a walk to check out the courts. The women will recognize me and ask about who you are. My last break-up was considered political roulette, so they'll be very intrigued."

"No wonder you want nothing to do with this scene."

"Thank you." Lacing her fingers through his, they followed the hostess to their seats.

Rory pulled out her chair and made sure to sit next to her, where he could hold her hand and face the other patrons. She wasn't sure if he noticed several heads turn as they made their way through the outdoor seating. When he leaned over and brushed a strand of hair out of her face, she guessed he was giving someone a show, but she didn't mind.

"You're better at this than you think," she said before their waiter arrived.

After ordering a few iced teas and sandwiches, Rory excused himself to check out the courts. In less than thirty seconds of pretending to look in her phone, one of the five women at the table nearby stood and walked over to Ainsley's table.

"My, my, Ainsley. Who is that gorgeous man you found, and does he have any brothers?"

The middle-aged woman's large diamond ring was evidence she shouldn't be worried about finding a man for herself, but marriages were like business deals in a political town.

"Mrs. Emily Monroe, shame on you. Last I heard, you were very happily married to the honorable Congressman from Alabama?"

Mrs. Monroe was political royalty in D.C., and she was the self-appointed queen of gossip. Ainsley knew she hit the jackpot of information as Mrs. Monroe took a seat next to her.

"Oh, I am still, but my younger sister just got divorced."

"Well, I just started seeing Rory, but he does have two equally gorgeous and single brothers." Ainsley looked around to see who else might be in earshot. "If you fill me in on everything I've missed in the last week at the club, I'll see if I can set your sister up on a hot date."

Ainsley knew she didn't need to beat around the bush with any number of her acquaintances at the club. The only thing they liked more than a juicy scandal was gossip. She had obtained more than one story over charity lunches with political spouses talking out of turn.

"Well, we've all been following the latest with your daddy's junior senator, Mr. Carter's attack at the park. You know, I thought it was a love affair gone wrong, but when the feds showed up here to question his wife Felicity Carter, we all realized it was much more serious."

"They were here? Did you overhear anything?"

"No, but you know Felicity was quick to try to explain her husband was not involved in anything unlawful," Mrs. Monroe said, rolling her eyes.

"I mean, of course she would say that," Ainsley said, waving her hand as if to dismiss the information.

Leaning forward, Mrs. Monroe looked around and

smiled a fake grin at a passing couple on their way to the courts before she whispered to Ainsley.

"You're right, of course. The only reason a wife would out her criminal husband would be to get rid of him. And from what I have gathered, it sounds like Mr. Carter has brokered a deal with the feds. Which means he must have been up to his eyeballs in some questionable scheme, and he isn't dumb enough to be a scapegoat."

"You really are the oracle in this town. A person can't have an affair, gamble their fortune, or pass a bill without you knowing," Ainsley said, hoping to stroke the woman's already-inflated ego.

"Now, you know this is off the record, but if you can use your journalism contacts to find out what Senator Carter was involved in, I sure would love for you to out him."

"You don't care for the Carters?"

"You know I like everyone, Ainsley, but sometimes, some folks need to remember their place in the hierarchy in this town. Frankly, I'm tired of Felicity copying my style." Ms. Monroe pushed out her flashy strappy sandals whose loud gold logo Ainsley should know but couldn't be bothered to follow. "I swear, every time I buy a new pair of shoes, the next week Felicity waltzes in with the same pair. I've tested the theory twice, and each time, there she is, poaching my look."

"You know what they say. Copying is a form of flattery."

"Honey, I didn't have kids for a reason. I don't need some younger, fitter mini-me waltzing around trying to steal my shine."

Ainsley forced a laugh as she caught Rory's eye. He was

talking to one of the tennis pros and seemed to be stalling to give her time to chat. She waved to indicate he could come back to his seat. She didn't see the senator's wife and guessed with the latest gossip about her husband cooperating with the feds, she wouldn't be showing her face any time soon.

"Oh look, that stunning man candy is heading back to you. I'd like to know more about how you met, but I'll wait until we can have more private girl talk."

Rory stepped closer and sat back down next to her.

"The tennis pro said he could work us into his schedule next weekend, if you're interested, baby," he said as he slid his arm around the back of Ainsley's chair.

With his other hand, he picked up the large iced tea she'd ordered him and took a long gulp. She and Ms. Monroe watched in appreciation as his carved jawline moved with each swallow. After draining half his glass, he pushed his sunglasses on top of his head and his eyes sparkled with mischief.

"Hello, you must be one of Ainsley's friends from college?" he said, reaching his hand out to Mrs. Monroe.

The woman's eyes fluttered as she pursed her lips in appreciation of the compliment that she looked much younger than she was.

"I see you have found yourself a real charmer, Ainsley." She shook his hand slowly as he gifted her a million-dollar smile.

"It is my pleasure to meet you, and if Ainsley is foolish enough to let you go, I have a younger sister that will be interested."

"Noted," he said but then set his eyes on Ainsley, and she

felt the heat in his knowing stare down to her core.

He knew she was attracted to him, and he was enjoying teasing her with pet names and intimate touches. With his hand behind her shoulders, he rubbed her neck, teasing his fingers into her hair.

"But I don't plan on letting Ainsley discard me anytime soon. I still have a few tricks up my sleeve." His eyes didn't budge, and she felt a blush push into her hairline.

"Mm-hmm, you two have fun. Ainsley, don't you forget about what we discussed. Remember to give credit where credit is due."

Tearing her eyes away from Rory, she smiled at Emily as she stood.

"Perhaps, a fun name for my favorite source."

"Something cuter than the oracle," Emily said before she strutted away.

Turning her eyes back on Rory, she expected him to break contact with her, but his hand continued to play at the nape of her neck as he perused the menu.

"Baby?" she whispered.

"Yes?"

"No, I mean, of all the nicknames you chose baby?"

His flirtatious eyes looked darker, like a large piece of jade as they settled on her.

"You don't like it? Too common for you?"

"No, I just didn't expect it. You strike me as more of a last-name-is-your-nickname kind of guy."

Leaning closer, his mouth skimmed her ear. "You're not one of my teammates, baby."

A shiver ran over her as his warm breath caressed her

neck. She wiggled in her seat just before his mouth pressed a kiss under her earlobe.

"I like your commitment to your craft," she said, turning to face him with little to no space between them.

"Well, we have to sell it, or someone is liable to think we just came here to snoop around."

His hand remained on the back of her neck as their server appeared, interrupting the intimacy they'd shared the moment before. She wondered if she imagined the pulsing heat between them.

After lunch, they hopped back in Rory's SUV where he'd left it near the valet. She felt the need to talk and occupy her mind before she got too distracted by the growing desire she had to kiss him again. He seemed completely unfazed by their time together and eventually she ran out of things to say. When she looked up, she recognized the winding road of Rock Creek Park and knew they weren't headed back to her place.

"Where are we going?"

"We need to confirm Senator Carter is cooperating with the feds or if that's just some bogus story he told his wife. If he is, it'd be nice to know who he's pointing the finger at." He glanced at her with concern. "If he's blaming your father, you'll need to decide if you'd rather break the story or protect your father."

Staring out the window, she knew he was right about her father, but there was no question of what she would do.

"You've been thinking about that while I've been babbling this entire time, haven't you?"

"Multitasking," he said.

A stone settled in her gut, because ever since visiting her father's office, she'd started to suspect he might be involved, but she didn't want to believe it. Her father was a self-made man. He prided himself on his honest work ethic and love of country. No matter how strained their relationship was, she knew he wasn't involved in any illegal activity. His patriotism was too strong for him to sell out his constituents or position in the government.

Chapter Eleven

Parking in front of an industrial brick building with the faded words *Paper Mill* running down the side, Rory texted his brother Conner to see if he was home. Ainsley had been quiet since he posed the question about what she would do if her father was involved—or worse—was being set up as the fall guy by his protégé.

Before he could figure out how to try to comfort her, his phone chimed several times in succession. His younger brother Conner was always sending what could be in one text, in multiple separate texts. In short, he was an antagonistic, unreformed class clown, and always way too playful.

Yo.
You need me to solve a big case?
Maybe take down a bank robber or save some kids?
I'm available in twenty.

He laughed at the four unnecessary texts and fired back a response before Conner could keep going.

I repeat, are you home?

There was a pause in his brother's response. If he had to guess, his brother was looking out the window on the sixth floor and spotted Rory's SUV.

Yes, come on up.
I'm bringing a guest, so make sure you're fully dressed this

time. He put away his phone and looked over at Ainsley, who was studying the building.

"Who lives here?"

"My brother Conner. He has a lot of connections with the feds. There's always another task force or big bust his unit is working on with federal agents. Nothing happens in this city without him knowing."

"Sounds like a great source for me to know, but why does he live in an old paper mill?" she asked.

"It's just an attempt by the builder to make an old facade trendy. If there is one diva in the Maguire family, it'd be Conner."

Checking his mirrors, he stepped out and walked around to open her door. At the first set of dark steel doors, he punched in a code, and the doors slid open. Next, he badged the concierge through a thick glass window, who gave him a thumbs up. Finally, at the elevator, he placed his palm on a screen, and the see-through glass doors slid open.

"Very posh for a cop."

"It gets worse. Don't let my brother's exterior fool you. He has a degree in finance and cashed in on the cryptocurrency movement early on."

After a short ride up, Rory stepped off of the elevator and held the doors open for her, ushering her to walk ahead. His brother's place had one unit per floor, and no one else could access it if they weren't on his guest list with their prints preloaded. To say he was security conscious was an understatement but working among motivated criminals for seven years left its mark.

When Conner's front door opened and he stepped out,

Ainsley stopped in her tracks.

Rory took in his brother's appearance: shaggy hair, a scraggly beard, and a thick muscular build dressed in paint-stained clothes.

"Rory," she called out just as he stepped up next to her, placing his arm around her shoulder.

"Sorry, I should have mentioned Conner does undercover work," Rory said.

When Conner smiled and his green eyes crinkled with mirth, his face transformed into the familiar boyish prankster.

"Your family get-togethers must be such a lively event," Ainsley said, sticking out her hand to greet Conner properly.

"You have no idea." Conner's deep voice was several octaves lower than Rory's, and Ainsley's big smile indicated she was impressed. "Ms. Nash, it's a pleasure to meet you. I hope my brother is using his pleasing manners with you. Our mom always had to spend extra time working with Rory on his abrasive tendencies."

Ainsley laughed.

"On the contrary, Rory's the nicest SWAT officer I've ever met, at least until Axe made me pancakes this morning."

When she smiled up at him, he tried to ignore Conner's arched eyebrow, indicating he spotted the vibe between them.

At some point since the gala, being with Ainsley didn't feel anything like work. He wasn't just enjoying her company. It was something more he didn't want to name.

"Are you going to let us in, or should we pretend to be comfortable in this concrete hallway?" Rory said, looking around. "Would it kill you to put up some art, maybe get a welcome mat?"

"Yes, it would destroy the unwelcome aesthetic I'm going for," Conner said, standing back and ushering them into his lair.

Inside there was a nice balance of industrial-style high ceilings with exposed vents and pipes, richly stained hardwood floors, plush rugs, and large deep blue sofas. Ainsley stopped after the entryway and took in the open concept. From the white marble counters, gray sleek cabinets, floor-to-ceiling windows on one entire side of the apartment, to the wall of books that framed a fireplace tall enough that she could stand inside it, the condo was very impressive.

"Can I just say you have exceptional style, and I need your interior designer," she said.

"Thank you, Ms. Nash. It's just my cozy place to get away from this crazy world." Conner sat down on one of the large sofas crossing his ankle over his knee and smiling from ear to ear.

"Please do not encourage him," Rory warned and ushered her to sit.

Deciding he needed some distance from her, he sat next to his brother, which only meant he was forced to watch her smile at Conner.

"My brother is going to try his best to embarrass me, but in the interest of time, let's cut to the chase," Rory said.

"Ah there he is. Control, precision, discipline," Conner said.

Ignoring his brother's attempt to mock him, Rory continued, "Conner, I assume since you knew who Ainsley was, you already know about this case I'm on?"

"Correct."

"While Ainsley's father, Senator Nash, alluded to a possible link between the recent attack on Senator Carter and the need for her protection detail, we're not convinced. However, yesterday someone was lurking in the garage at Ainsley's building, so we thought we'd gather more information and make our own assessment."

"Got it," Conner said. "Typically, if a woman has a man lurking in her garage, my first question would be who is the last person you had sex with?"

"Conner," Rory barked.

"Excuse me?" Ainsley said as heat flooded her cheeks.

If he wasn't so annoyed with his brother's line of questioning, he might enjoy the pink in her cheeks and how bright her eyes looked with surprise.

"But since your father requested the protection, we have to assume the threat is related to him or his work in some way." Conner looked from Ainsley to Rory.

"Then we don't need to review my sex life?" she said, clearing her throat.

Conner nodded. "Correct. The other option is your story about insider trading has your father worried someone will try to shut you up."

"I never actually named who sponsored those environmental bills or the investors in the companies involved," Ainsley said. "My network didn't want to get caught up in a defamation lawsuit. We knew after naming the companies involved, someone else would start digging and fill in the blanks."

"Well, whoever is involved may assume you'll figure it out and wish to avoid you outing them. As an unnamed source, I can tell you the word is Senator Carter sang like a bird to the feds after someone tuned him up in the park last week."

"So he is cooperating with the feds?" Ainsley said.

"What I don't know is if he named your dad as being involved. The fact that your father requested protection for you makes him look a little guilty," Conner said.

"Right."

"Or he isn't involved and wasn't sure who was, but he wanted to make sure no one could hurt his family," Rory offered.

"You know I usually deal with gang turf wars and drug dealers, but sometimes these guys punish their own to set an example. I think whoever had Senator Carter jumped, miscalculated. It was like a warning that he needed to stay in line or he would be sacrificed, but most white-collar criminals buckle the second violence is introduced," Conner offered.

"So Senator Carter is making a deal to save himself, but who is he going to point the finger at?" Rory mumbled aloud, brainstorming the possibility as he paced in front of the fireplace.

"He does this. It's part of his process," Conner said.

"I'm learning," Ainsley said.

"I'd like to believe your father didn't know his junior senator was up to his neck in shit," Conner said. "But how well do you know your father's dealings?"

"Our relationship is strained. My parents have had an

empty marriage since I was a kid. My father was always working or traveling for work, building his empire. He only ran for the Senate when his colleague told him he couldn't do any better than the cheats in Washington. When he won the Senate seat, he became obsessed with the game of politics. Outsmarting his opponents and changing hearts and minds."

Rory looked at Conner. "I don't think the senator is involved, but he must have suspected it was close to home. I bet that's why he requested the D.C. metro police provide protection, not the Capitol agents," Rory said.

"You're giving my dad a lot of credit."

"No one amasses your father's wealth and success without having the ability to be several steps ahead of their competition, or in this case, enemy," Conner said.

"We don't have enough information to narrow down a suspect, and I bet Senator Carter's lawyers will be working out a deal for weeks," Rory said.

"Someone is going to break this story before Senator Carter finalizes his deal. This story is too juicy," Ainsley said.

"Maybe reporting on what you know so far will help flush out another clue," Conner said.

"People are naturally going to look at the other senators from New York who worked with Carter, your dad included," Rory said. "I think you need to have a conversation with him before you take this story live."

"I know. I just don't want to give him the opportunity to try to interfere. What if he is involved?"

"Only one way to find out," Rory said.

Clapping his hands together, Conner stood up from the

couch.

"Whelp, you didn't need me to help you figure that out, but it was a nice break from sitting in a crack house waiting to score," Conner said.

"You do that?" Ainsley asked.

"Connie works in the narcotics unit, but not for much longer. He's up for promotion soon."

Rory was proud of his younger brother's efforts against the never-ending battle of drug activity in their city. But he'd be happy once his brother put the undercover work behind him. It was too risky.

"Mom will be relieved when you start showing up for Sunday dinner, looking more like the pretty boy she raised and less like one of her clients."

Conner grinned. "Speaking of, are you going tonight?"

Rory looked at his watch. It was only three o'clock, and technically he could drop Ainsley off at her place and let Jake or Axe take over the evening shift.

"I didn't plan on it. I'm trying to limit the number of teammates on this one," Rory said, making up an excuse.

"Why don't you just bring Ainsley? There will be plenty of firepower."

"I wouldn't want to intrude," Ainsley said, standing up.

The idea of joining him for family dinner was probably the last thing she wanted to do after spending most of the last forty-eight hours with him.

"Are you kidding? Three unmarried sons and her only daughter off in New York? Mom will love to have you over. She may not let you leave," Conner said, looking at his watch.

"We'll see," Rory said in a noncommittal tone.

"Great, I'll see you both there in a few hours. Maybe I'll even clean myself up a bit." Conner pretended to smooth his wild hair back and produced another charming smile for Ainsley.

"Don't worry, you're safe as long as you stick to him like glue," Conner said as he put his arm around Ainsley to walk her out.

Clearing his throat, Rory followed them. "Thanks for letting us stop by."

"Seven sharp," he said, hugging Rory at the door. "See you soon, Ainsley," he called down the hall as Rory walked her to the elevator.

Then they were alone in the glass elevator, and Rory couldn't help but stare at the grin on her face. Which is why he saw the exact moment it fell.

"Are you okay?" He lifted her chin, so she was forced to look at him.

"I hadn't considered that the story I'm covering could be linked to real danger. I assumed there was no threat, and this was all cooked up by my father's office to slow down my story."

"You know, the fastest way to find out what your dad knows is to ask him."

"I'm not sure he would tell me, and meeting with him alone is going to be tough. I wasn't exaggerating when I said he is always working."

She sounded less resistant to the idea than she had earlier.

"I'll try to get in touch with him without his staff intercepting it and set something up," he said.

"Okay, and you'll go with me?" she said.

"Of course."

Back in his SUV, they were both quiet, and he mulled over everything they'd discovered as he drove them to her place. When she'd talked about her dad, she'd sounded way more hurt than mad at their contentious relationship. Hopefully, for her sake, her dad wasn't involved in any part of the insider trading, but innocence wouldn't guarantee their safety.

"I feel safer with you around," she said, breaking the silence as he pulled into the garage of her building and parked. "But I'd hate to keep you from your family dinner. You should go. I'm sure Jake or Axe could manage here for a few hours without you."

"I'll go to my family's dinner on one condition." He pinned her with his eyes. "If you agree to go with me. After that gala and yoga, the least you could do is tag along for one of my events."

"Will you tell your parents I'm a protectee or your date?"

"I wouldn't lie to either of my folks, besides they'd sniff it out in a heartbeat."

"Too bad. I enjoy pretending with you."

Their eyes locked. But then he remembered there was a possible viable threat of someone wanting to hurt Ainsley to either shut down her story, put pressure on her father, or both. Breaking eye contact, he scanned the garage and spotted Axe by the entrance with his SUV backed in so he had eyes on the entire area. He flashed his brights, and Axe replied with his.

"All clear. Let's get you upstairs. You're going to need to rest before a night with my family."

"So Conner is the charming, outgoing brother. You're the quiet and controlled one. Your sister is the only girl, so probably the bossy princess. What does that make your youngest brother?"

"The baby."

"I thought I was the baby?" she teased as they entered the foyer of her building.

Smiling he nodded, "you're a different kind of baby."

He wondered how reasonable it was for him to resist the attraction he felt toward her. He'd even started to consider asking her out on a proper date when the case ended, but what did he have to offer a woman like her beyond a physical connection that would likely rival any relationship he'd ever had? As cliché as it sounded, she was from a different world growing up in mansions with the glamour of a millionaire family. But he'd be damned if he wasn't going to enjoy the time he had with her now.

Chapter Twelve

L OOKING DOWN AT her dark, skinny blue jeans she'd paired with a lightweight powder blue V-neck sweater, Ainsley debated on booties or trendy sneakers. What did a protectee wear to a family dinner with the smoking hot SWAT officer assigned to protect her?

The brown booties gave her a little extra height, so she opted for those, zipped each side, and grabbed her bag before she could second guess herself.

Rory was waiting in the living room, still dressed in his casual clothes from their lunch at the tennis club. She wondered where he was keeping his gun.

"Are you sure you don't mind being subjected to a family dinner? My mom will latch onto you the minute we arrive." His handsome brow furrowed.

"I'm looking forward to it. I'm curious about your parents and how they managed to raise four of you and stay sane."

Rory unfolded from his seat with a huff. "That journalistic mind of yours trying to figure me out?"

"No, just genuine curiosity." She moved toward the foyer, where her coat hung in the closet next to Rory's. She liked the look of them mingling together. Plucking his black police-issued coat off the hanger, she handed it to him. He was standing close and reached into the closet to retrieve her heaviest coat, then held it open to help her put it on.

"Quite the gentleman bodyguard."

"It's going to be cold out by the fire pit, so you'll need this extra warmth," he said as his hands wrapped her coat around her, but he was careful not to touch her.

"A fire pit sounds like a treat. Will there be s'mores too?"

"Maybe if you behave and don't encourage my brother's misbehavior."

"I would never dream of that," she said, even as her lips spread in a big grin.

"Just as I suspected, it will be three to one tonight. I'm just grateful my sister is out of town." Rory tapped a button on his radio. "I'm bringing Flash down, is everything clear?" He paused and waited for Axel to respond.

"Did you give me a codename?"

Rory nodded. "Standard."

"Flash as in I'm flashy, or flash of the limelight?" she said, waiting for Rory to go out into the hall first.

"Afraid that's classified," he said with a big smile.

She wondered if she could convince him to hang out with her after his assignment ended.

"Ready?" he asked after checking the hallway.

"Are you?"

She followed him into the hall and locked her door. Once downstairs, Jake was waiting in an SUV for them.

"Everyone ready to get their eat on?" Jake said as they got settled in the backseat. "Mrs. Maguire is almost as good of a lawyer as she is a cook."

"Your mom is a lawyer? How did your sister avoid the law?" Ainsley asked, pretending she hadn't Googled the Maguire clan the second night Rory was assigned to protect her.

"She's our black sheep," Rory said. "My parents knew early on Charlotte was more of a creative, analytical type. She works in marketing and PR. I don't think either one of them minded when she didn't want to pick up a badge or defend thugs."

"Your mom is a defense attorney?"

"She was a local district attorney. Then last year received her judge appointment. She claims she wants to retire soon."

"Quite a pedigree," Ainsley said.

Rory smiled with obvious pride, and his dimple made an appearance, digging into his left cheek.

"You should smile more." The words were out before she remembered there was a third wheel in the car.

Jake coughed over a laugh and cleared his throat while Rory shot daggers from his narrowed eyes toward the front seat.

"Sorry to interrupt, but did you tell your dad we're bringing company?" Jake asked as he maneuvered through the city traffic and merged onto the highway along the Potomac.

Ainsley looked out at the water and listened to them talk shop.

"He must have spoken to Conner because he called me about twenty minutes after our meeting and told me this was the one time I was allowed to bring my work home with me." Rory caught her eye in the dimming light.

Jake laughed. "Papa Maguire isn't going to mind being included in a little police work. He misses it too much. I hope he warned your mom because if we arrive and she thinks Ainsley is your girlfriend, she could be too disappointed to make dessert." Jake continued to laugh as Rory's cheek flexed and his lips pressed together in a grimace.

Her stomach fluttered at the thought of being Rory's girlfriend. How many previous women had he taken home to meet his parents and how would she measure up?

"Maybe this is a bad idea," she said, looking at him.

"Too late now." Jake pulled into a quiet suburb where there were white picket fences, tree swings, and old two-story brick homes with big front porches. They moved slowly down a long driveway of a white Victorian-style home with a detached garage and a beat-up basketball hoop hanging above. Ainsley spied a backyard oasis with Adirondack chairs that surrounded a fire pit and Edison lights hanging above pavers that lead to a wide staircase. There was a large outdoor cooking area and a tall man with salt and pepper hair manning the grill. His size matched Rory's but with less defined muscles. Ainsley smiled, looking up at Rory as he held her door open. Axe ambled down the driveway, having backed his car in to face the street.

Jake beat them into the yard and was hugging a slight woman with thick auburn hair that bordered on unruly. The woman spotted Ainsley and pushed Jake aside.

"Rory, is this your special guest? Your father was very tight-lipped about who you were bringing. Now I can see why." She stood up on her tiptoes to kiss Rory's cheek with one eye still on Ainsley.

Rory's hand settled on the small of Ainsley's back protectively, and she couldn't help but wish she was meeting his parents under different circumstances.

"Mom, this is Ainsley. She's the subject of a protection detail, and after an eventful weekend, we thought a Maguire family dinner would be fitting."

"Oh my, Ainsley. That doesn't sound like a great reason to spend time with these boys. I'm sorry to hear how you met, but I'm happy you're here."

"It's nice to meet you, Mrs. Maguire."

His mom's smile grew. "You're just as beautiful and poised in person as when I see you on TV. No doubt you're using those investigative skills to keep Rory's team on their toes."

His mom wrapped an arm around her tenderly, and the woman's warmth was like a salve on a wound she didn't know she needed. Tears pricked her eyes at the thought of her mom and how aloof and unaffectionate she could be. As a child, her dad had always been the one ready with a hug, but they'd grown apart.

"Thank you, Mrs. Maguire, for letting me invade your family dinner."

"Nonsense. Just like these two hooligans, you're welcome here anytime. With or without Rory. Although I don't know why you wouldn't want his company."

"Mom," Rory said in warning.

"It's a mother's right to brag about her oldest, single, handsome son," his mother said with pride.

Ainsley couldn't help but chuckle as Rory hung his head in defeat.

"Sorry," she whispered, nudging his side.

"Oh, this is just the beginning," he replied with a bashful smile.

"Ms. Nash, welcome, dear. You just take a load off. You'll be more than safe here," Rory's dad said, rubbing her arm before turning to Rory. "Son, I was just telling Jake we can test out the new perimeter fence I installed. It's electric." Mr. Maguire's eyes lit with excitement as he showed Rory a screen on his phone that mapped out the lawn perimeter with circular sensors glowing.

"Dad, if you add any more gadgets to this compound, you'll need a second generator," Rory said.

"See why I'm thrilled to have another woman in the house tonight? Come on, we need to escape fast." Rory's mom hooked her arm through Ainsely's and pulled her close. "You're saving me from all the police shop talk."

They walked up the steps together, but Ainsley glanced over her shoulder and found Rory's eyes on her. He nodded approval with a slight grin of encouragement. She knew he meant to indicate she was safe, but it felt more intimate than a bodyguard's approval.

Rory's mom held the screen door for her and ushered her into an inviting sitting room with wide plank wood floors, overstuffed beige couches, and high brown leather-backed recliners. A brick fireplace commanded one wall with large lanterns on the hearth filled with candles lit inside. It looked like the sitting room out of a Southern Living blog post.

"You have a beautiful home. It feels so cozy," Ainsley said, walking beyond the living room into a large kitchen with tall white cabinets and a large butcher-block island with a farm-style sink inlaid.

"Please call me Cora. At work I'm Mrs. Maguire. At home, I'm Mom or Cora."

A tinge of sadness washed over Ainsley at the lack of having such a comforting relationship with either of her parents. She was close to her sister, but they were always playing phone tag and Amelia traveled a lot for work as a model.

"How are you holding up? I can't imagine having to trust strangers with my safety. Where is your family?"

"You know, initially I wasn't too worried, and I kind of enjoyed having Rory around. He's so serious all the time. I like to try to loosen him up."

His mom looked up from the fragrant basil she was chopping with a smirk.

"When we met, he made it clear he wasn't happy about being stuck with me, which made it more fun to annoy him."

Cora laughed.

"I think we both thought it was unnecessary and would be short-lived."

"But then," Cora prompted as she pulled open the oven to check the bubbling dish inside.

The smell of roasted garlic and tomatoes filled the room.

"And then Rory chased a man down that was hanging out in the garage of my building but wasn't able to catch him."

"What does Rory say?"

"I think he's frustrated he has to babysit me, but he seems very dedicated to his work."

"His career, following in generations of Maguire men's

footsteps, has been his sole focus for as long as I can remember." Cora leaned against the counter and looked away from Ainsley with a frown. "But he grew more intense after a terrible incident a few years back."

"He told me what happened."

Cora's head popped up, and she stopped her chopping. "He did? Huh, he's usually very private about it."

Before she could dwell on that comment, Axe walked in.

"Judge, I'm here to officially act as a taste tester, slicer, and lookout," Axel said with a big grin. Right behind him, Conner walked in with a bottle of wine. His scraggly beard was still crazy, and she realized his wild hair matched his mom's auburn color. Since she had seen him, he'd attempted to comb and slick back the thick locks but failed miserably.

"Mom, you wouldn't pick this stray dog over your own most beloved son," Conner teased, kissing his mother's cheek. "Good evening, Ms. Ainsley. It's nice to see you again." He winked at her as if he could read her thoughts.

"It is a hard job to be surrounded by so many attractive, cheeky young men, and normally, I would enjoy this game but tonight Rory brought me a companion. So both of you scram." Cora used her dishtowel to swipe at both of them, but not before Axe dug into a bag of shredded cheese on the counter. "Go."

Conner nudged her shoulder. "It was worth a shot. Just remember whose idea it was for Ainsley to join us when you're slicing that cake. You're welcome in advance," he called, leaving the kitchen with Axe in a headlock.

"I'm starting to wonder if we missed out on more fun in my house growing up with no brothers."

"Well, nail polish, dance parties, and girl talk are also loads of fun. Thankfully, I had my Charlotte to keep me company."

Ainsley walked over to a counter where Conner set the wine to see a framed photo of the Maguire family. Rory stood with what looked like a forced smile in the back, and a pretty woman with equally wild auburn hair sat with Cora's hands on her shoulders. There were no spouses, just the four kids and their parents.

"You have a beautiful family."

"Thank you. Why don't you open that bottle Conner brought us? He may look like a vagabond, but he has very good taste."

After pouring them each a glass, Ainsley was put to work. She removed the large lasagna from the oven and helped Cora make a salad while several loaves of bread warmed up in the oven. Next, they frosted a large chocolate cake and left it on display on the counter. She was enjoying the warmth of the wine and Cora's company when Rory walked in. He leaned on the counter next to where she stood, and a look passed between him and his mother before he spoke.

"Everything okay in here?" He studied Ainsley, and her cheeks warmed under his scrutiny.

"Yes, we're just getting to know each other. I may trade your brother Finn in and adopt Ainsley," Cora said, interrupting their staring contest.

"Where is he, anyway?"

Cora shrugged. "We didn't see him very much when he lived here and even less now that he rented a place near school. I think he's still coping with everything."

"I'll give him a call, Mom, and try to see him this week," Rory said.

Cora moved around the counter with the salad and handed it to Rory before patting his cheek. "Thank you."

Ainsley listened intently but didn't want to pry.

Rory put the salad on the table and filled the water glasses without being asked. Ainsley found herself watching his every move and didn't notice Conner had rejoined them and stood next to her.

"Mm-hmm," Conner hummed at Ainsley with a knowing look. He caught her checking out Rory and smirked. "Mom, I think we should adopt Ainsley too. She smells better than Finn. Rory, let's arm wrestle to see who gets to sit next to her."

"Don't you start, Conner. No wrestling tonight. I won't have you scaring her off," Cora said.

"Start what? It's not my fault women naturally find me more affable. Rory's too serious. Women want to laugh. Right, Ainsley?" Conner put his arm around her shoulders, coaxing a laugh out of her without even trying. "See?"

Rory set the water pitcher down on the counter before pulling the bread from the oven. He helped his mom without being told what to do, and she wondered if he was closer to his mom even though he followed in his father's footsteps.

"Hands off the protectee, Conner, or I'll have to assume you're a threat." Rory set the hot baking sheet down and punched Conner in the side.

Conner let out a grunt before moving to clutch his side dramatically. "Mom, Rory punched me."

"Oh, work it out, boys, but if either of you scare her off, I'll never forgive you," Cora said as she carried the large lasagna to the middle of the table. "Now, let's eat."

Ainsley watched as Cora moved to the screen door and hollered out it was dinnertime. Conner took a seat at the table and pointed at the seat next to him. Rory dipped his head toward her ear.

"Thanks for humoring her. She's eager for one of her sons to settle down so she won't be so outnumbered."

"Maybe you should. You're not getting any younger," she teased and bumped his leg with her hip. "If you didn't work so much, you might find time to meet your soulmate."

Rory filled her glass of wine back up while he considered her comment. "I was hoping she would find me first."

"How's that working out for you?"

Everyone else arrived from outside and took their seats, but she was enjoying their intimate bubble in the warm kitchen.

"Jury's still out," Rory said. "Come on, you must be hungry after today."

There were two empty seats at the table left for her and Rory. She picked up her glass and moved to take the seat next to Cora.

Rory followed and pulled out her chair before taking his seat. His dad led them in a prayer where everyone held hands, and when she put her palm in Rory's, the electricity was off the charts. He squeezed her hand before letting go, and the conversation at the table took over.

After dinner, they all gathered around the backyard fire pit. Rory took turns with Jake and Axe, who were each manning the front and back gates to have a break. She didn't know where they each went when they said they were doing a loop but assumed they were checking the street or fence line.

At ten, Rory tapped his watch. "We better hit the road. The ladies both have work tomorrow, and we have team-mates to relieve us back at the nest."

Cora wrapped up some leftovers and then gathered Ains-ley in a big hug. "I hope to see you back here again for family dinner but not as a protectee," she whispered in her ear.

Ainsley thanked his parents and followed Rory's lead to the vehicle. She took his hand when he offered it to help her step up into the backseat and felt the jolt of energy between them again. Instead of joining her, he closed her door and got in the driver's seat. His gorgeous profile was marred by a clench of his jaw as they waited for Jake to get in the car too. She wondered why he chose not to sit with her but guessed he wanted some space from the rising tension between them. He had a job to do. She was appreciative of his diligence but didn't think she could resist the pull she felt toward him much longer.

Chapter Thirteen

THE NEXT MORNING, Rory tried to use a hot shower to wake up. Although he'd left Ainsley's place at midnight while another teammate stood watch, he still didn't get much sleep. He'd never dealt with being attracted to someone at work, much less the subject of a case. Of course, there were attractive female cops, paramedics, and lawyers he met over the years, but he'd never been distracted by them.

He'd never wished for a do-over on how he met someone before, but he couldn't help but want one with Ainsley.

What if they'd met at their favorite coffee shop or on the street? Would they have just passed each other by? It was impossible to tell if the rising connection between them was because of the circumstances or a real raw attraction. And even though he was extremely attracted to Ainsley, he still wasn't interested in a relationship. His job required too much of his focus. At the same time, he couldn't get the memory of Ainsley's lips, so soft and full, out of his mind. He wanted to know everything about her, starting with how her skin would feel against his without any clothes to separate them.

The problem wasn't how they met. The problem was he was pretty sure she was the type of woman that dated a different kind of man, and he didn't have the space in his life for the attention she would need.

The fact that they came from totally different backgrounds was just the easiest reason to discount any attraction. She came from privilege and the kind of wealth that always flew first class, never needed to save up for a new stove, or worry about retirement. Not that Ainsley acted snobby in any way. If he had to guess, she didn't accept a dime of money from her father. But it wasn't her socioeconomic status. It was her glamour. She was stunning, poised, and driven.

There was no way her goals included settling down with someone that would have to work nights and weekends. She was the kind of woman that married a man with a private jet and probably several homes. The kind of man who could work a few hours a day, if at all, and make enough money to take her on international vacations every season.

Cutting off the hot water in the shower, he stood under the stream of now-cooling water, letting it turn ice cold before he shut it off. He needed to wake up and stop thinking about the kind of man Ainsley would marry and worry more about the people who might threaten her safety.

Just because she made the best of being stuck with him all weekend and was nice to his family at Sunday dinner didn't mean they were even compatible.

Just because he felt drawn to her didn't mean she felt anything remotely similar.

And this was why he couldn't get into anything close to a real relationship. It was too distracting, and he needed to focus on keeping her safe and figuring out who her father was worried about. He'd managed to speak to her dad the night before, during one of his rounds of checking on the exterior of the house, and he agreed to meet them after the morning session and several meetings on the Hill. Her father had been clear from the onset that Rory shouldn't trust anyone and only communicate with him via his private number. Rory hadn't mentioned it before to Ainsley because he didn't want her to be upset or jump to any conclusions.

He planned to get back to Ainsley's in time to take her to work, until his phone started blowing up with messages.

My office, 0830. Don't be late. Captain Sullivan's name flashed on his screen.

The boss is looking for you, and two SUVs with Capitol agents just pulled into guest parking, Jake texted.

Damn, I'm on my way. Can you get to Ainsley's?

After texting Axe that his shift was going to be a little longer, he drove to the office in record time.

Unease settled in his gut as he entered Captain Sullivan's office. Senator Nash's chief of staff, Paul Jenkins, and the lead Capitol agent in charge of the senator's protective detail were already there. It was clear Jenkins was running the show, and there was still no detail offered about the threat. D.C. Metro was being directed to drop the protection detail and leave Ainsley's safety to the Capitol agents. Once the meeting ended and Jenkins and the agent departed, Rory pressed his captain for more details. She assured him if she knew, she would tell him.

"I'm sitting on a lot of unused leave hours. I think I'll cash in a week or two," he said to his captain.

She nodded while crossing her arms over her chest. "You

plan to leave Jake in charge, or is he going to take some leave also?" she asked.

"He can manage the team while I'm out. It'll be good practice for him," Rory said, trying not to smile.

"Does that mean you're taking the job at training?"

"You said I had until Friday to decide. I'm still thinking it over."

"Okay, Maguire. Just remember where your jurisdiction ends, and if you're doing a moonlighting job, you need to report it through proper channels."

"Of course, Captain. I don't plan on doing anything but maybe a little fishing with the old man and eating too much home cooking."

Her smile indicated she knew he was full of shit before she turned toward her computer screen. "Tell the commissioner I send my regards."

"Will do," he said, exiting her office.

His dad had been Captain Sullivan's boss when she was a new officer with D.C. Metro, and most times, his family ties worked in his favor.

Ainsley was clear she wanted him to stick around, and he needed to know she would be safe. If the Capitol agents wanted to stand guard outside her apartment, it was fine by him, but he planned to be as close to Ainsley as he could. He needed to know who was involved in the possible threat against her and why. If her father's office was involved in the insider trading, he didn't believe it was the senator. He knew for a fact the senator had called the police commissioner himself to request D.C. Metro provide security for his daughter, so why was Jenkins the one visiting his captain to end the protection detail? Did Senator Nash even know the security had been called off?

After the meeting, he went straight to Ainsley's news network, where he found Jake outside her office.

"No new details, other than our protection assignment is done. Supposedly, the Capitol agents are going to take over. I convinced the captain to give us the rest of the day to make sure Ainsley has a chance to hire her own private security if she wants."

"You don't think they have any intention of providing her protection, but she needs it?"

"Probably. Listen, I put in for two weeks of leave. I need you to lead the team while I'm out."

"No problem. You just be safe and call us if you need backup," Jake said. "I'll let Axe know he can go home and rest."

"Thanks," Rory said.

"Be safe, brother," Jake said, dapping Rory's fist.

Being on a tactical team often felt like a brotherhood. The men and women were physically tough, but it also took a level of trust and communication to work efficiently together. It was developed over time and created a bond beyond simple friendship. They trusted each other with their lives. It would be hard to walk away from the team.

Knocking on Ainsley's closed door, he opened it to poke his head inside.

Her eyes landed on him, and her scowl changed into a big grin that felt like the sun breaking through a dark and stormy sky.

"You're back?" she said, coming around her desk to sit

on the edge.

He walked in and closed the door.

"I'm back, but we need to talk."

"You're not staying?" she asked, not hiding her concern.

"That's up to you. Technically, today at nine a.m., we were pulled off your protection detail."

"Oh."

She looked defeated.

"I told Jake to stay until I arrived. I wanted to see if the Capitol agents were going to assign anyone, but it doesn't look like they have plans to."

"So whatever the threat was, it's magically gone? It seems odd my dad would call off the details without even telling me."

"The thing is, I'm not sure your dad even knows that they ended the protection," Rory said, pausing to study her reaction. "His Chief of Staff was meeting with my captain when I arrived."

"Jenkins? I'm starting to think all roads lead to him. What if he's the one behind the attack on Senator Carter? He could easily influence a bill for the Senate to push. The staff are the ones that do a lot of the leg work, and everyone is on an environmental kick. He could have just latched onto a bill that was already being proposed and created a few companies that could supposedly do some of the work," Ainsley said, grabbing a file from her desk.

"Which would mean your dad wasn't involved, but I bet he had his suspicions when he ordered your protection."

"We need to talk to my dad before my segment at five. I need another source before I implicate my father's chief of staff."

"I have a meeting set up with your dad for lunch," Rory said.

He knew this information might not land well and was prepared for her to be upset.

"You've been in touch with my dad?"

"He phoned me directly the first day. He asked that I report to him with any concerns. Now I can't help but wonder if he meant if your story got you too close to the truth. He made it clear he didn't want anyone to know we were communicating."

He could see the wheels in her mind spinning, but she wasn't upset.

"What if Senator Carter isn't the only one working with the feds?"

Before Rory could respond, an alarm began to sound, and a robotic voice came over the loudspeakers.

"A fire has been detected in the building. Please proceed to the nearest exit." The recording was on a loop and repeated.

Rory didn't hesitate. "Grab what you need. We're leaving."

"It's just a fire drill, and all my notes are on that board," she said, pointing to her murder wall of sticky notes and markers scribbled on a whiteboard.

Pulling out his phone, he took a picture.

"Your protection detail ended an hour ago, and you're supposed to go on air in fifteen minutes with a teaser on a story that implicates the man that canceled your protection. Now there is a fire drill?" Rory posed the scenario, and her eyes grew big.

"There's no such thing as coincidences," Ainsley said. Then she grabbed a few notes off her desk, stuffed them in her bag, and took his hand.

"Stay close?" Rory said.

"Gladly," she breathed, weaving her fingers through his and pulling her body closer to him.

A twinge of desire pushed through the adrenaline that started pumping the minute the alarm went off. But he needed to focus on getting her out of the building. Slowly opening her door, the smell of smoke hung in the air and red lights flashed as the electronic voice overhead continued. Half her office was already emptied, and everyone was heading toward the east side exit. He pulled her in the opposite direction.

Chapter Fourteen

A FTER EXITING THE building via the rear service stairwell, Rory's truck sat in the adjacent parking lot illegally parked. All the fire trucks and activity were on the front side of the building. Once they were both in the SUV, she let out the breath she'd been holding, and he drove in the opposite direction of the noise.

"You know I can't just sit on this story, right?" Ainsley said.

"Yes, but we need to make sure we do this in a smart way. So you'll be safe and get your big story."

"We? Didn't you say your department was told to stand down on my protection?"

His brow furrowed, and he ran his hand through his messy hair again, distracting her with his sexy, disheveled look.

"Yes, but I don't think the Capitol agents had any intention of providing you protection, and even if they did, your father's chief of staff likely would know where. Assuming he's involved and your story implicates him, you'd be a sitting duck."

"So I'm on my own?" she said, starting to panic.

"No, I'll stay with you until we figure out who is involved. Once your story is out, the FBI will have to arrest them."

"You're going to voluntarily help me? Won't you be risking your job? We don't know how far this corruption goes."

"I took some vacation time," he said casually. "I'm so entrenched in this police force between my dad and uncle's tenures; you don't need to worry about me."

"Oh." Her brain wasn't working, and her mouth was spread wide in a big smile at the thought that he wanted to help her.

"The question is, what do you plan to do next? You've been chasing a big scandalous story so you could run with what you have, but you'd be leaving several fill-in-the-blanks."

"And a lot of people will point the finger at my father, if I don't give them somewhere else to look. If my father isn't cooperating with the feds, they're probably already looking at him. That weasel Jenkins could be setting my dad up."

Rory was quiet and let her consider her options.

She had two sources to back her guess about the junior senator turning state's evidence against someone. But if she wanted her story to garner national attention, she couldn't do that with innuendos. She needed to figure out who was behind the insider trading scheme and provide proof. It might also be the only way to protect her father's good reputation.

"What time is the meeting with my father?"

Rory's carved jaw and full lips spread in a smile.

"In about thirty minutes, your dad said to use the garden gate at his brownstone."

"Since when do you and my dad have private meetings?"

"Since I'm the man protecting his daughter, I guess," Rory said. "He might be surprised when we both show up."

"Tough."

✕

ONCE HER DAD'S shock wore off that she voluntarily sought him out, he ushered them through the house to his study. Rory offered to give them space, but she didn't want him to miss any details. She felt like they were a team, and she valued his input.

Her dad's home was huge and immaculate, but it felt empty. The study was the only room that oozed cozy and reminded her of the office he had when she was little. After school, she would find him working, and she would go through his books or set up her coloring books on his chess table. He'd been living in D.C. for ten years since he started his political career, and she'd only been there a few times before.

"Why are you home in the middle of the day, and where is your security detail?" Ainsley asked.

"I feigned an upset stomach when Rory called this morning for a meeting. The Capitol detail always stays in a car out front, but Frank is just in the kitchen, always ready for a surprise." Her dad's butler/personal bodyguard had been working for him since his days in New York; she'd almost forgotten he was staff, after seeing him for most of her life.

She walked farther into the room to sit in one of the plush leather chairs, and her father chose the matching one next to her. Rory sat a little farther away on a matching Chesterfield sofa.

"I'm happy to see you, Ainsley. I've been worried, but I knew I could trust the commissioner to put his best officer on this." Her dad smiled at Rory.

It seemed like such a change from the last time they all met in her father's office, and she realized her dad must have been testing Rory.

"I'm sorry, Dad." Her shoulders dropped from the tension she'd been feeling. "I thought you were just trying to keep me away from a great story because you or one of your political friends were involved in something shady."

Her dad shrugged. "I guess I can't blame you. It does look really bad for me and my office at this point."

The pain in his eyes was unmistakable, and a twinge of guilt formed like a brick in her stomach. Only she knew he didn't deserve her pity. He proved his disloyalty when she was twelve, the first time she met one of his girlfriends. How was she supposed to give him the benefit of the doubt after years of deception?

His frown deepened before he leaned closer, as if he were going to reach out to her, and she instinctively sat back. He let out a breath that seemed to release all the tension in his shoulders.

"It's my fault you could think I was capable of something like that. I never should have agreed to your mother's terms."

"What do you mean, Mom's terms?" She crossed her legs and tried to project a calm she wasn't feeling. She only had a few hours before she was due to go on air and wanted to be ready to deliver the last segment of her story. The final blow to the man that set up an elaborate insider trader scheme and betrayed her father. But she needed her dad to fill in a few blanks.

"We agreed to never tell you and your sister about the terms once it was clear our marriage ended. Your mom was adamant that you girls should always believe we had a loving marriage that faded with time, but the truth was..." He hesitated.

The emotion in his eyes made him look years older, and she realized he was sad.

"Are you saying you and Mom agreed to stay together for the kids? Because I'm pretty sure that's been proven to backfire since the 1960s."

Her dad's smile didn't meet his eyes.

Rory sat quietly on an adjoining couch with his hands steepled and his head down.

"Your mother was enchanting when I met her. Gorgeous, of course. She was fashion's muse, the Italian siren splashed on every magazine, walking in every major fashion show. And she set her eyes on me. At first, I assumed it was my money, and she wasn't the first woman to be intoxicated by my black card. But she was different. She made pasta from scratch in her lingerie, and baked cookies. She doted on me and spoiled me. She didn't want the material things I could offer, or at least it wasn't her goal. Sure, she wore the jewelry I would buy to impress her, but she wasn't greedy for it."

"She was in love with you."

"She was in love with the power. She wanted the status, the respect that me and my family name provided."

"Dad, that's ridiculous. Mom came from a good Italian family. Poppi's winery has produced successful vintages for fifty years."

"That's true, but the winery was on a much smaller scale before your mother began to make serious money modeling. Then she pumped her assets into the family business once we were married."

"But she doesn't even stay in D.C. with you. She never attends any political events anymore. Did she get tired of the social scene or your philandering?"

His sigh of resignation made her feel bad for being so blunt.

"No, she hasn't needed to tie herself to me since you girls were little. She's enjoyed the power of the Nash name for decades. By the time you were born, she'd already entrenched herself in New York society. She's fashion royalty with an American lineage that can be traced back to the founders of our nation. She hasn't needed me for years."

"You're saying she used you?"

"Your mother treated me well in the beginning, and she gave me two wonderful children. She supported me. She even encouraged me to pursue politics. She just never loved me, not in the way I loved her."

Ainsley sat back as if he'd struck her. Memories of her parents' interactions played in her mind. She couldn't recall her mom ever gushing over her father or even saying I love you. She remembered her mom didn't bat an eye when Ainsley was eighteen and challenged her to acknowledge her father had a girlfriend right under her nose. At the time, she thought her mom was trying to be strong and not fall apart when she'd been fine with their arrangement. Hell, it sounded like it was her plan all along.

"You married her for love, and she married you for your name?" she asked.

It was like her entire life was being flipped upside down. All this time, she thought her father had bailed on their family when it had been by design. Her mom had pushed him away.

"To be fair, your mother never promised to be anything more than she was. She was the perfect spouse for events: intelligent, worldly, spoke three languages, hosted magnificent events, and could schmooze business associates and politicians. She had her career, came from a good family, and was beautiful. She could have picked any man with a fortune. It was too easy to fall in love with her, and I never stopped to consider that she didn't love me in return. We were married after a year of dating, and you were born the year after that. We were ecstatic. Then your sister came along, and your mom said everything was perfect. I hoped to have one or two more kids, but let's face it, the woman has to do all the physical labor that first year so I didn't push her when she said she didn't want any more. I had you girls and your mom. I was happy."

He stood and poured them each a splash of scotch, then held up the bottle to Rory to see if he wanted any, but with a nod, he indicated he didn't.

"You were happy until what?" She had to know what changed, what pushed him into a line of mistresses.

"When Amelia turned two your mother said she needed space," he said.

After accepting a glass from her dad, she took a hearty sip of the amber liquid and let the smooth oak-infused flavor roll down her throat. The burn was muted by the hints of vanilla.

"Mom ended your marriage when I was five? But we stayed in New York. We all lived together for another thirteen years."

Her dad's blue eyes creased on the edges as his smile pushed laugh lines into his chiseled cheeks. "I wasn't going to be deprived of seeing you girls grow up, just because your mother didn't want me. I wasn't going to be some every-other-weekend type of father. I enjoyed going to your recitals, basketball games, spelling bees, and parent-teacher nights. Do you remember?"

"Yes, you rarely missed an event," she said.

He nodded. "You girls didn't want your old man around once you hit your teenage years, but that wasn't going to stop me from being there. I can see now I made one huge mistake in ever letting you think I was the one at fault." He scoffed before finishing off his scotch. "I thought I was being the chivalrous man, letting your mother save face with you both. If one of us had to be the bad guy, I let it be me. But now you hate me, and you're too focused on work to have a relationship. Amelia falls in love with any man that spews adoration on her, and the Lord knows you're both too beautiful for your own good. Just like your mother."

His eyes softened when he spoke about her mom, and she couldn't believe she never realized before that it wasn't out of respect or deference.

"You're still in love with Mom, even after all this time."

He nodded. "I'll always be in love with your mother, and that's okay. I'm just sorry I ever let you think I wasn't."

"Why didn't Mom love you back?"

"You can't force someone to love you, any more than you can stop yourself from loving someone you shouldn't. I think in her way your mom cared for me as much as she was capable, but I don't think she's ever found her true love."

Hot tears rolled down her cheeks, and the anger she held against her father for so long dissolved into guilt. For years, she had punished him for running out on her mom, when in reality, he'd been pushed away. Worse, her mom had let her hate him. Her dad's strong hand enveloped hers, and he squeezed it.

"It's not your fault, Ainsley. I should have told you years ago. I should have told you when you were eighteen, and you discovered I had a mistress."

"You should have, but I don't know what's worse, thinking your dad is cheating on your mom or knowing your mom never loved your father and pushed him away."

"Maybe now we can start over," he said. "I'm not perfect, but I'm not nearly as terrible as we let you think."

Laughing through tears was the kind of emotion that felt too overwhelming. She wished Rory could hold her through the wave, but their relationship was nothing more than a work assignment up until now. It'd be a little odd if she just crawled in his lap for comfort. She avoided meeting his eyes but could swear they were on her.

Leaning forward, her dad gave her hand another squeeze and handed her a few tissues.

"Now that we have that all out on the table, who else do

you think is behind this plot? Because I think I've narrowed it down."

"I'll give you one guess," she said, squeezing his hand back.

"Jenkins," they both said at the same time.

Rory smiled, and she felt the warmth in his eyes from across the room.

"Senator, I don't mean to be crass, but do you have any proof against Jenkins? If not, I think you better get your attorneys involved, and I should probably not be a part of this conversation."

Her dad stood and pulled a big book off one of the built-in shelves along one wall. What looked like an old atlas was an empty wooden box, and inside, her father had several paper files.

"I met with an FBI agent a few weeks ago to explain the fraud I uncovered between Jenkins and Senator Carter. They keep saying they're getting closer to an arrest. But then Senator Carter was attacked, and I worried Jenkins and whoever he may be working with got wind of the investigation."

"So you let Jenkins think you requested the protection for Ainsley because Senator Carter was your junior State representative," Rory said. "Smart."

"I want to report all of this: Jenkins' involvement, Senator Carter's, and your innocence. But a few protected sources won't be believable because you're my father. People will assume I'm just protecting you."

"My attorney assures me I'm protected not only as a whistleblower but because there is no evidence linking me to

Jenkin's scheme. He was meticulous in keeping me out of the bill preparation, and I can prove from records on the Hill that I was in ethics meetings when this bill was being worked. Jenkins knew I would never condone his get-rich scheme, but Senator Carter was more malleable."

"Chances are this wasn't Jenkin's first dalliance into white-collar crimes. He may have far more to lose than we know. Which makes him very dangerous," Rory said.

Her dad nodded. "Which is why I'm hoping you'll continue to protect Ainsley, Sergeant Maguire."

"I plan to sir, but we also need to make sure you're safe until Ainsley can get enough attention on this case. Once the real proof is out, the FBI will be forced to arrest Jenkins, and I'll bet his cronies will be happy to make him the scapegoat."

"It's all in that file. You can use all of it, Ainsley, and you can name me as a source if needed. But I think you'll find more than enough there. My lawyer has already filed a civil suit documenting the evidence. Which also makes it public record if one knows what to ask for."

"You knew I wasn't going to stop digging, but you couldn't tell me all of this in your office with Jenkins watching. Very sneaky, Dad."

"You can't be successful in business or politics without learning to avoid the snakes in the grass."

Chapter Fifteen

AFTER POURING OVER all the documents her father gave her, it was obvious Jenkins was linked to everything. The LLCs for several of the environmental construction companies were in his name or some variation of it, his bank accounts were linked to dozens of trades, and he'd drafted the bill on his office computer. Jenkins should have known that any number of government officials could access the records of files on his publicly appointed position. Everything went into the archives.

It always amazed her how arrogant people could be. As for Senator Carter, he was also up to his neck in dirty trades, and he had been the person pushing the bill Jenkins drafted to get as many senators as possible to sign off. What wasn't clear was who went along with the bill to get in on the insider trading and who thought they were doing something good for the environment. But as she reported in her half-hour, dedicated segment that evening, the trades would prove who was involved in the fraud, because money did not lie.

Once the hot lights of the sound stage dimmed, she took a big breath. Rory stood in the shadows, watching over her the entire time. The big smile on his face told her she'd done a good job. The best part had been the footage of Jenkins getting arrested during the middle of her broadcast. It was like the feds and the news gods had smiled down on her.

Before she could walk over to Rory, her producer was popping a bottle of champagne, and everyone was clapping. It was probably the best moment she'd had in her career so far. Finally, when the celebration wound down, she walked over to Rory.

"That was pretty fun to watch live," he said as one hand fell to the small of her back. "Congratulations."

"Thanks. What now?" she said.

"Good question. I'll make sure you get home safe, and then I guess we'll see. I did promise your dad." That was all he said, but at least he didn't seem ready to end their time together, either.

✕

THE ADRENALINE OF the day was catching up to her, and fatigue was crawling in as they walked into her office to gather her things.

"I doubt you need my protection anymore with Jenkins' arrest, but you might need my help to get away from the paparazzi," Rory said, looking down at the news trucks outside her network's building.

She peeked over his shoulder and couldn't help but laugh. "That has to be a first. Reporters chasing another reporter at a different network for a story."

Turning toward her, the limited space between them vanished.

"How does it feel? You got your big story, next, fame and fortune."

"It feels like now I'll need an even bigger story."

"How about we start with a big meal and a good night's sleep?"

"You sure you don't mind taking me home? You're technically off the job now," she asked, grabbing her things.

"Shhh don't tell anyone, then I can enjoy some time off."

"If you're avoiding going back to work, I'll happily be your make-believe assignment. It's the least I can do after you protected me and helped me with the biggest story of my career."

"I was thinking of maybe getting out of town for a few days, since I already took the week off. I have a cabin out at Lake Anne I try to get to a few times a year."

"A cabin sounds like a perfect escape from the city." She tried not to sound too disappointed that their time together was ending.

Turning from the window, he stood a few feet away with his feet wide, arms crossed and self-assured.

"Maybe you should come with me. Let something else take over the news cycle," he suggested.

Her skin prickled with desire, and she wanted to scream, "Take me now."

Instead, the question on her lips was, why was he asking her? Was he interested in spending time with her at his lake cabin, or was he just being the upstanding guy she knew he was and offering her help? But she wasn't sure she would like the answer. She didn't want to hear about duty, or his compulsion to help people. She wanted him to want her.

"Hmmm, stay locked up in my apartment or spend a few days at your cozy lake cabin with you? Such a tough decision."

His eyes squinted. "Don't make me second guess the offer."

She walked closer and crossed her arms to mimic his posture.

"Are you sure you're up for a few more days with me?"

"I can handle it, but my cabin may not be the type of vacation destination you're used to."

"If it's anything like your designer home, I'm sure I'll be comfortable. Besides, it'll give me time to work on my pitch for a national news correspondent gig," she said with a smile.

"So that's your big goal, to land a new job?" Rory asked, as he led her out of her office to the elevator.

She hesitated, wondering if it was disappointment she heard in his voice.

"A bigger correspondent job was always the goal. This story could make my career. If my segment gets enough interest, I could be looking at offers from other networks and in bigger cities."

He nodded and pressed the button for the garage where he'd parked.

Looking up, she realized how little they knew about each other.

"Getting chosen for a news correspondent position in New York is the golden ring I've been chasing ever since I graduated from journalism school."

"Good for you. I hope it's everything you dreamed of once you get there." His smile looked forced, and his sad eyes had her second-guessing if New York would live up to the hype she'd built it to be.

"Ya, I think it's important to have a goal to work toward, but I guess sometimes life changes during the journey."

"You're an impressive woman," he said, helping her into his SUV.

There was unabashed admiration in his eyes, and she squirmed under his praise. Her skin warmed, and the urge to reach out and touch him was strong. She felt like she lost her voice as she stared into his eyes. She wanted to bridge the weirdness between them but also didn't want to misread him.

"Are you hungry?" he asked, breaking the silence.

"Starving. There's a good Thai place down the road from my place that delivers. It's my favorite."

"Perfect. Thai is my favorite, too," he said.

Meeting his eyes, butterflies in her empty stomach felt like a herd of elephants stomping. She was alone with her bodyguard, and all she could think about was how she wanted him to kiss her. Instead, she swung her legs into her seat and waited for him to hop in.

He easily navigated his way through the city while she called in their order. They picked up the food and then sat in companionable silence as evening darkened the streets, like a couple used to spending time together.

"So how did your captain respond when you said you were taking time off to babysit me?"

"The last time I took more than a long weekend was when my little brother Finn was wounded in action and sent to a hospital in Germany to recover. That was five years ago.

Trust me, I have plenty of time to burn."

"Was your brother okay?"

"If you consider shamelessly flirting with his German nursing staff and sneaking out to the bars a week after he arrived okay, yes."

Laughing, she wondered if a playful sense of humor had been hiding under his serious demeanor this entire time. She'd seen little flashes of a different version of him but on rare occasions and they didn't last long.

"Finn is fearless and got lucky it was nothing more serious."

"I see heroism runs in the Maguire family."

After picking up their food and parking in her building, they rode up to her condo, and relief washed over her. She'd started the day not sure how things were going to pan out. Now her story was wrapped up, her relationship with her father was starting over, and Rory was still with her. She was exhausted, but nervous excitement still coursed through her limbs.

They sat at the kitchen counter, and each enjoyed large plates of curry, rice, and drunken noodles.

"Oh my gosh, I don't think I realized how hungry I was until a few bites ago." She groaned at the deliciousness of the buttery, spicy sauce.

When she opened her eyes again, the look of pure desire in Rory's eyes was unmistakable. Reaching across the space between them, he used his knuckle to wipe the side of her mouth where some of the sauce had landed. She watched, riveted, as he brought his hand back to his mouth and licked the juice he just removed from her face.

She gulped down her water, but it didn't quench the thirst that settled low between her legs.

"Good, right?" she asked.

Her voice sounded strained, and by the sly smile that spread on his mouth, he heard it too.

Now that he wasn't technically working, they were spending time together by choice. It seemed like a big step, but there was still a barrier between them, like an invisible line they both had to cross if they were going to explore the attraction between them.

Before he could respond, her phone began to ring incessantly with bells she had set on it. Her producer's name flashed on the screen.

"I better take that," she said, wishing instead he would throw her phone across the room and take her on the kitchen counter.

He just smiled big, pushing his dimple deeper. She could get used to seeing him smile.

Chapter Sixteen

T HE NEXT MORNING, Rory sat reading the newspaper in Ainsley's living room. The night before had ended differently than he expected. After taking a call from her producer, Ainsley had gone to her room to change, but when she didn't come back out to the living room, he checked on her and found her fully dressed laying on her still-made bed with her phone in her hand. He hadn't had the heart to wake her to even get into pajamas. He decided to just stay at her place for the night to make sure she was comfortable being alone again. Although he was serious about his invitation to join him at his cabin, in the light of morning, he didn't think she would take him up on the offer. She'd just landed the biggest story of her career. She would probably be fielding requests for interviews and multiple job offers.

It was nearly nine a.m., and she was still asleep, which was surprising with the aromatic smell of the freshly brewed coffee he'd made. Clearly, the last few days had worn her out. During their short time together, he'd learned she was an early riser and required coffee first thing in the morning. Collapsing the newspaper he'd taken from her front door, he heard a door swing open.

"Good morning," she said, walking down the hall. "I was

worried you would be gone."

Her smile felt like a wall of lights, warming him from across the room.

"Nope, just waiting for you to wake up. I took a shower in the guest room. I hope you don't mind." He held up the paper. "You're bigger than D.C. famous now."

The national paper he held up had a huge front-page picture of Jenkins getting arrested, and her face in the corner. The headline read, "D.C. Reporter Unearths Scandal in the Trenches."

"Wow, that is a big picture."

"I'd like your autograph before I go, and I think the paparazzi figured out where you live. There were half a dozen outside when I stepped out on the deck."

"Oh, I'm sorry I fell asleep last night. I don't even remember crashing."

Laughing, he stood and handed her the newspaper, then brought her a cup of coffee.

"When I didn't hear from you again, I peeked in to check on you and found you out cold. Your producer was still yammering, so I told him you'd call him back this morning."

"So pathetic. Our first chance to hang out, and I passed out." She hung her head.

"You had a big day."

"Am I still invited to the cabin?" she asked.

Surprise was mixed with relief that she wanted to spend more time with him. He had no idea what that meant, but he wasn't ready to say goodbye either.

"Absolutely, if you're sure you can get away for a day or

two."

"One hundred percent. Just give me a few minutes to pack some things, and we can go."

✕

"WHAT EXACTLY IS that man's job?" Ainsley asked while pushing a cart into the women's clothing section of a super-store thirty minutes outside of Alexandria. "He just smiled and said hello when we walked in. I feel like I should have tipped him."

"I think his official title is greeter," Rory said, trying not to laugh.

They needed a few groceries and supplies before arriving at his cabin where there was only one small store with odd hours. He fought the urge to laugh at Ainsley's constant look of awe as she took in all the large displays and low prices on goods.

"They sell pork rinds, women's panties, flip-flops for two bucks, and they pay someone an hourly wage for hospitali-ty?" she said.

"Our cart is getting pretty full, so it must be working."

They'd only stopped to get a few fresh groceries and things he knew he needed for the upkeep. But she'd admit-ted to never having been in a superstore before and grabbed several items off of enD.C.aps in the first ten feet. Chips, cookies, sparkling water, and bug spray sat in the large cart already. Now she was working her way through the women's clothing section.

"True." Ainsley stopped to admire a black-and-white

checkered-patterned, long cardigan.

"Get it." Rory plucked the hanger from her and laid it in the cart. "It gets cold in the evening by the lake."

"Your cabin sits on the lake? Will I need a bathing suit?" she asked.

Her eyes widened, and a small smile pushed at the corner of her mouth. The urge to kiss her was so strong he didn't realize he'd taken a step closer until her hand was on his forearm.

"The lake is still too cold. We just need enough groceries for a few days."

"What are the odds they have organic chia pudding here?" she asked.

Clearly, she wasn't worried about the sexual tension that had just been flowing between them. But he couldn't figure out if she wanted to go with him to avoid all the media buzz, to spend time with him, or if she was still worried about Jenkins.

"I think you may have to settle for oatmeal, non-organic."

"I never settle."

She took the cart and pushed it through the rest of the women's section, getting distracted with each new area. Sunglasses, an adult onesie, jean leggings, and she stopped to spend far too long comparing cotton thongs with hip huggers.

"Don't you need anything?" she asked as they passed the men's section.

"No, I have a wardrobe at the cabin year-round."

"Do you spend a lot of time at the lake?"

"Ever since I was a kid, my family spent several weeks in the summer and any long holiday weekend we could at the lake."

"We're staying in your family's lake house?"

"No, a few years ago, I got a great deal on a dilapidated cabin. It's a work in progress, but there is running water." He managed to keep a straight face as her nose scrunched with distaste.

Finally, they walked into the grocery store portion of the megastore, and the lower temperature helped him cool off until he noticed Ainsley's nipples perk up through the thin fabric of her dress. She was looking at the bags of lettuce trying to decide which to buy while he was having visions of pulling her wrap dress down her shoulders in the produce aisle. He wanted to warm her skin with his mouth and tease her as much as her body was taunting him.

"Do you care about spinach mix or spring mix?"

"Either is fine," he said.

She reared back at the sound of his curt tone.

"Are you having buyer's remorse about bringing me?"

"Spinach mix," he said, tossing a bag in their cart. "We need to get back on the road so there's still some daylight to deal with any unforeseen surprises at the cabin."

"I guess if this rustic cabin doesn't have electricity, we can use each other's body heat to stay warm," she teased.

"Let's go," he said before he started pushing the cart toward the front of the store.

He could hear her chuckling as she caught up to him.

On the rest of their drive, she peppered him with questions about his family and childhood. She probably knew more about him than all of the women he dated over the last decade combined, and for some reason, he didn't mind opening up to her. An hour later, he pulled down the curvy driveway to stop in front of his cabin. Turning off the truck, he looked over to see her response.

"You call this dilapidated?" she said, opening her car door.

The afternoon sun glinted off the water casting a spotlight on the whitewashed stone-and-log cabin that sat on the edge of the lake, nestled between tall trees, with blue shutters, a stone chimney, and a red door.

"You should have seen it a few years ago. I've made a lot of improvements, but it may not be up to your standards."

"Just because I'm a city girl doesn't mean I've never been glamping."

With a laugh, he gathered as many bags as he could, which was everything she bought and the leather duffel bag she'd packed.

She beat him to the door and turned to find him with his hands full.

"Where's the key?"

She reached out to slide her hand into his pocket before he could set any bags down. Only the thin pocket material stood between her touch and his leg until she gripped the keys. Her pursed lips proved she was enjoying her ability to torture him.

"Oh, got 'em," she breathed before turning away to unlock the door.

"It's the one with the American flag on it," he said, trying to sound unaffected by her touch.

"Your slice of the American dream?" She opened the door and stepped inside. "Oh, it's perfect."

New wide plank wood floors, lightly stained, gleamed in the sunlight coming in through the skylights he'd put in the new roof last summer. Setting all the bags down, he punched in the security code to turn off the silent alarm he always used between visits.

"A big comfy couch, floor to ceiling built-in bookshelves, and a rustic brick fireplace with a thick shag rug. Can we stay forever?"

Smiling, he enjoyed her approval and noticed the minute she spotted the modern kitchen.

But the real clincher was the back wall sliding glass doors looking out onto the lake.

She ran her hand along the back of the couch as she made her way farther inside but stopped to stare out at the backyard.

"You can open it up and have a look," he said, placing the groceries on the counter.

Unbolting the glass door, she walked out onto the deck. There were a few chairs, then steps led to the lush green lawn with tall grass and wildflowers. The lake looked like glass reflecting the tall trees in the late afternoon sun like a mirror.

"It's not much, but it's mine," he said from the deck. She stood a few feet away in the grass, staring out at the water. For some reason, it was important for her to like it. He wanted her to be comfortable, but there was something else.

"So this is your happy place," she said, walking back up the steps to stand next to him.

"Ya, I guess it is. Whenever I get a day off, I come here.

Shift work is grueling so it's nice to come here to escape."

They stood there for a bit, both taking in nature and leaning on the railing where their elbows just barely touched.

"I guess having to babysit me is adding to your terrible hours?"

"Maybe I'll put you to work on one of my cabin projects as payback."

"Thank you for bringing me here," she said, not able to look away from the majestic view.

Staring at her profile, he was struck again by how enticing she was. Slender curves, thick dark hair, and plump, kissable lips. But she wasn't his to have. She was chasing a dream in New York, and he was on the fence about leaving the team.

But what if they could just have now? Was that why she'd wanted to come with him?

She turned to face him, her brown eyes studying him. "Your grimace is back."

"I was just thinking I don't have to work for the next week. I should be thanking you."

"Well, I'll try to make sure I have some threat to my safety once a year so we can come out to the cabin. Your annual vacation will be my retreat."

She rested her hand on his arm, and his attraction toward her hummed just under the surface. He could swear she felt it too. She'd kissed him at the gala, then again in his house. The way her gaze darted to his lips made him think she wanted to test out an idea on him. But when she moved past him back inside, he second-guessed what they were both doing. Maybe she wasn't as interested as she seemed when there was an element of danger, or maybe she never was.

Following her inside, he decided to give her some space.

"I'm just going to do a loop around the house, and I need to turn on the water. Then I'll show you to your room."

By the time he made sure there were no problems inside or outside the house and had the water turned on, Ainsley had put away the groceries. He found her checking out his spices and pulling a few down for what he guessed were her plans for dinner. He moved to stand next to her to test the kitchen sink, and after a few seconds, the water started flowing.

"Can I ask you a silly question?" she said.

"Do I have a choice?"

"Why were you willing to let me join you here? I probably could have hired some security in D.C. to help me navigate the paparazzi until they got bored with me. Why would you waste your leave on babysitting me?"

His jaw clenched. He knew the question lingered between them, and he didn't have a great answer. Instead of facing her, he walked past her up the open staircase.

"I think it's your sparkling personality," he teased, and she hustled to catch up to him.

"Come on, I'll show you your room," he said, not looking back.

Once up the steps, the loft opened into a large room with more wood floors covered by a thick, geometric gray-and-blue rug, a rustic wooden dresser stained in a whitewash with matching nightstands, and a huge bed. There was only a sheet draped over the bed, and she hung back by the entrance.

"Don't worry, I keep the bedding in the closet so it doesn't get dusty in between my visits.

"But this looks like the master bedroom?"

"You'll have a private bathroom up here, and this is the nicest room. Also, it's the safest because you're elevated from the ground floor. I'll take the guest room downstairs."

"Okay, when you put it like that."

Her smile looked forced, and he wondered if the room was too bare.

"I can't remember the last time I took a real vacation where all you do is relax and recharge. I'm not sure I know what to do with myself," she said.

The line between them had blurred. He wanted to stay close to her, but she didn't need his protection now that her story was out. Now they were just two single adults with unresolved sexual tension.

"I think the tub in the bathroom might help you remember," he said.

Her eyes grew wide. "Do tell."

He walked through the arched doorway into the master bathroom, which was rustic and manly. There was a deep metal tub that looked like it belonged in an old castle, one large sink in a slab of black granite perched on a wood vanity, a circular bronze framed mirror, and a glass-enclosed shower lined in herringbone tile with flecks of gold.

Ainsley was still stuck on the massive tub he'd found at an antique store.

"The queen called, and she wants her tub back," she joked. "This is amazing." Walking closer, she straddled the side of the tub to step inside, sat down, and rested her head on the slanted edge that flared up to her shoulders. "Why didn't we get bubble bath soap?"

Her long lashes fluttered on her upper cheeks, and she let out a deep breath.

"I'm glad you approve."

"There is enough room for two, in case I'm in danger of drowning," she said.

Her eyes didn't open, but her mouth spread with a wide amused smile.

Leaning forward, he hovered over her close enough to count the freckles along the bridge of her nose. Her eyes popped open, and her perfect pink lips spread with a gasp. She couldn't back away but didn't try to.

"Tempting," was all he managed over the lust that was tightening his throat. Then with one last look, he walked out of the bathroom.

✕

AFTER WHAT COULD only be described as a romantic dinner for two, while watching the sunset, Ainsley fielded several calls from her producer.

"I'm sorry. I told them I need a day off, but they want me to record a few teasers for my story they plan to repackage for the week. I guess Jenkins and Senator Carter have court dates, and they want to milk the coverage."

"It's fine. You don't want to lose the momentum on this," he said, forcing his disappointment away.

Back on her phone, she fired off a few texts then set the

phone aside and picked up her wine glass.

"I also don't want to miss this sunset." She stood up. "Want to go outside?"

They sipped their wine while watching the rest of the sun disappear, and several solar-powered lights turned on along the path down to the small dock he had along the lake. Fireflies flickered in the trees, and he let out a deep breath he didn't realize he'd been holding.

"Is there another reason you wanted to get a week away from work?"

"I was offered a job as director of our training unit, but I'm on the fence about leaving the SWAT team."

"Sounds like an important position, but a big change for you."

"My captain wants an answer by Friday."

Before she could say anything else, her phone started ringing from inside.

"Go on, take care of your work. The lake will be here tomorrow."

"Thanks." She hurried inside and took her phone upstairs.

After putting away the leftovers, he made a small fire in the living room. The question she asked him earlier still rang in his mind. Why did he volunteer to take leave and protect her? But the exhaustion of several days caught up to him, and he must have fallen asleep. He woke to the sound of Ainsley calling his name in a panic.

"Rory, I think I heard something."

He sat straight up and reached for his gun, but it wasn't on his hip. Looking around, he was disoriented in the dimly lit room but then remembered they were at the cabin.

Ainsley's bare legs were pressed against the stair railing, and the moonlight made her t-shirt translucent. Her tousled hair hung over her shoulder where she leaned forward. The patter of feet sounded from the back deck, and he was forced to turn away from her ethereal figure.

"What did you hear?" he whispered, moving closer to the back of the house.

"A rustling sound and then a bang." Her breathing was heavy.

"Stay there. I'm going to look out the back. I'm guessing it's just a raccoon or a bear passing through."

"A bear?" her voice whisper-squeaked in panic.

Walking through the kitchen, he heard a rattling sound on the side of the house. He'd never seen a bear this close to the cabin, and he hadn't put any trash out so he didn't expect there to be any animals sniffing around.

Being careful to stay along the walls, he peeked out the back and saw a shadow on the deck. Moving closer, he heard a light tapping noise, then saw a black nose press against the glass door, as two pointy furry ears came into view. A coyote stood on the other side of the glass. It wasn't very big, but it seemed daring to be on the deck. He wondered if it could smell them from when they sat outside earlier. Flipping on the floodlights he'd installed, he watched the animal start to back away. When he tapped at the glass, it bolted, and he watched it move to the wooded area to the right of his property. Was that the last they would see of the nocturnal animal?

Grabbing a glass of water, he made his way upstairs, but

Ainsley wasn't standing at the railing anymore. He couldn't see her in the dark until his eyes adjusted again, and he found her sitting in his bed with the covers pulled up over her head.

"It was nothing. It's safe to come out."

He couldn't hide the humor from his voice.

Pulling down the covers, she blew at the hair that fell in her face. She looked sexy and cozy at the same time.

"What was it?"

She sat back against the low headboard and pulled the covers back up to her neck.

"It was only a coyote," he said, taking a long sip of the water.

He suddenly felt very parched. Like a thirsty man who knew water wasn't what he wanted, but he drank it anyway before setting it on the nightstand.

She dropped the covers down onto her lap. "Only a coyote? Was it frothing at the mouth? Did it have blood on its fur? Can it get in here?"

Laughter pulled at his mouth. "No, no, and no. If I'd thought it was rabid, I would have shot it."

"How are you so calm? Do you always see coyotes here? What if it comes back in the morning?"

"I've never seen a coyote this close to the cabin, but I assure you, it was more afraid of me than we should be of it. It probably caught our scent earlier and wanted to investigate. They don't like to be near people. You're perfectly safe."

She took a deep breath before plucking the water off the nightstand and chugging the rest.

"Fine, but you're sleeping with me tonight."

"I don't think that's necessary. Even if we had a pack of coyotes, which we don't, they can't pick locks. They can't break in. You're safe inside."

She cringed and pulled the covers up closer.

"Just for tonight. I'll never sleep if you make me stay by myself. We both know they'll sniff me out as the weakest link and eat me first."

He would have laughed if she hadn't legitimately looked completely freaked out. Hunkering down in her covers, he could tell she wasn't going to be deterred.

"Fine, but scoot over. You're on my side."

"My side is in the middle," she said, moving about two inches.

He couldn't believe he was now going to be forced to sleep with the most desirable woman he had ever met and not touch her. He should be recommended for sainthood after this.

"I won't even hog the covers," she whispered as she lay back half on his pillow.

"Scoot over more, and I need my own pillow."

Lifting the covers, he slid into the low bed and tried squeezing his eyes shut as her soft body pressed against his side. She faced him, and one hand looped over his bicep. He was just going to try to pretend she wasn't there. Even though he could feel her breath hit his shoulder, and her scent had already invaded his senses. Soon the heat they created in the bed together had him moving the blanket farther down his chest. He'd rather sleep without his shirt on but didn't want to create an awkward situation.

"I noticed you're in exceptionally good shape but no visible tattoos?" she whispered.

"How do you know I don't have one on my ass?"

He felt the bed move from her laughter, and it relieved some of the tension he was feeling.

"Why have you been hiding this sense of humor?" she whispered.

His breath caught in his chest, and for some reason her innocent question made him think of Sam. His life had changed so drastically when his best friend was shot and killed. Initially, he had to deal with the aftermath of the crime and then the fallout within his family of losing one of their own, a young husband, brother-in-law, son-in-law, and best friend. Rory had put up walls, and in a lot of ways, he never let them down.

"I guess when it comes to work, I learned it's safer to remain focused and serious."

Her hand moved to his bicep, and her fingers traced over the scar. Her touch was light where the skin lost sensitivity. But then she pushed her hand under his arm to loop around his chest, and she pulled herself closer to him, eliminating the space between them.

"You're not at work anymore. You can be yourself with me now." Her voice was muted from behind him where her mouth was pressed close to his shoulder. "But for the record, I do like having your protective instinct around to scare away the coyotes and bad guys. It's nice to feel so safe."

He could hear the sleepiness in her tone and guessed she'd been up all night working until the sounds outside spooked her. As much as he wanted to roll over and ravage her, she hadn't invited him into bed for that. She needed to feel safe and comforted, and maybe he did too. Taking another deep breath, he gripped her hand in his and listened as her breathing grew heavier. He wanted to bridge the gap between them but wasn't sure if she wanted something more than friendship. She was chasing her big dream job in New York, and he wasn't looking for anything serious, but if she wanted to take a piece of him with her, he was more than willing to let her.

×

IN THE MORNING as his eyes adjusted to the sunshine peeking through the thin curtains, he heard Ainsley's deep breathing behind him. Laying on his side, facing away from her hadn't deterred her from getting as close to him as possible. One arm was still draped over his chest, and she managed to push one leg through both of his, like a human pretzel. He could feel every inch of her body pressed against his, causing his desire for her to rage. Meanwhile, she slept. Taking a deep breath, he slowly disentangled himself and tucked her back into the covers. Her dark hair was splayed out on the pillow, and her pink lips were slightly parted. He couldn't help but smile at the idea that he got to sleep with Ainsley Nash yet didn't touch her. The guys on the team would never let him live it down if they knew.

Grabbing a sweatshirt from his dresser, he made his way to the kitchen and started the coffee. There was a morning chill out on the deck, but no sign of the coyote. Part of him hoped the mutt made another appearance so Ainsley would ask him to sleep in her bed again.

The lake was covered in the morning fog. Dew blanketed the grass, and it was cold enough for him to pull up his hoodie. Would Ainsley balk at helping in the yard, or was she planning to work all day? The next question died on his lips when he looked up to find her walking toward him in her sneakers and her sleep shirt. She had a blanket wrapped around her shoulders and two cups of coffee in her hands.

"Good morning," she said, handing him a cup.

"How did you sleep?" he asked, sipping the coffee and letting the hot liquid punish him for what he wanted to ask her.

"Fantastic, actually." She looked around cautiously. "You're sure we don't need to worry about the wildlife?"

"Yes, but let's get back inside. It's too cold for no pants."

Standing in the narrow kitchen, it dawned on him that he wasn't very good at one-on-ones with gorgeous women when he wasn't charged with protecting them.

"So what's the plan for us today?" she asked.

He stood with his back against the kitchen counter, and she leaned against the other side, sipping her coffee.

"That depends on you. I have a fun day planned of mowing the grass, cutting some firewood, cleaning out the gutters, and maybe cutting some of that brush back." He pointed to the closest part of the forest that seemed to be encroaching on his land.

"Okay." She gulped another sip of coffee.

"Unless you changed your mind, and your producer convinced you to hightail it back to the city."

That would cement the fact that they were never meant

to have anything.

"When I woke up in your bed, it struck me that it was the first time I've felt so safe and relaxed since all this started."

"Oh." He didn't know where this was going.

"I sent my producer several pre-recorded blurbs he asked for, and then I told him I was turning off my phone for the next twenty-four hours."

"What if there is an emergency back home?"

"My dad will call you. Otherwise, I am off the grid with you."

Her smile lit up the room, and he didn't know if he could be a perfect gentleman for the next twenty-four hours.

"So, what should we do together? Last night you passed out. Then I passed out, but now we're both rested," she said.

Clearing his throat, he couldn't tell if there was an invitation in her question. "Cabin chores are always first, then we can have some fun on the lake. I have a canoe and can take you out on the water."

A smile spread on her face. "That sounds great, but first, I'm making us breakfast."

Her t-shirt rode up her legs as she bent down into the fridge to retrieve the eggs.

Taking in the view of her muscular calves and beautiful natural tan was nearly his breaking point. Turning around abruptly, he cursed.

"I'm going to get the ladder to start cleaning out the gutters and haul out the lawnmower."

"Okay, I'll whip up something in about fifteen minutes."

He took a big gulp of his coffee before heading back outside. The cool air was only going to help him so much. Twenty-four hours of not making a move suddenly sounded impossible. If she just wanted to spend time with him to feel safe, he didn't want to ruin it by hitting on her, but he was almost positive there was desire behind her smiles. He just needed to confirm she was attracted to him without offending her.

Chapter Seventeen

BEATING EGGS WHILE she stared out the window above the sink, Ainsley watched as Rory's back muscles flexed with each swing of an ax. His strong hands gripped the handle and the force split the wood instantly. If she didn't know any better, she would think he was working off some frustration, but she seemed to be the only one experiencing the sexual tension between them. That morning when she found his side of the bed empty, she was annoyed. At first, she thought maybe he was trying to be respectful, but then the idea he wasn't attracted to her took root.

He had been a perfect gentleman when she paraded him around as her boyfriend at the charity gala, and he never once crossed the line when he slept in her house every night.

But she thought she caught him checking her out more than once since they'd met, and the energy between them always felt charged. He was off the clock now and invited her to spend a few days with him at his remote, cozy, cabin. In return, she was going to use every opportunity to flirt with him. She needed to know if he was just as attracted to her as she was to him and why he wouldn't act on it.

Ten minutes later, when he walked in with his arms full of wood, there was a sheen of sweat on his brow, dirt on his arms, and he'd never looked sexier.

"Breakfast is ready," she said with a smile.

"Great, let me just put this away."

"You must have central heat since it's not freezing in here."

"I do, but it's always good to be prepared."

She finished setting the small table and made them both a plate, eggs, bacon, and toast. She found jam in the cupboard along with other basic staples. Once he walked back into the kitchen, his manly scent invaded the space.

"This kitchen is cozy," she said, bumping his hips at the sink where he was scrubbing his arms and hands clean.

He scooted over to give her space to fill two glasses with ice water, and she could feel the heat rolling off of him. His jaw flexed, and his back looked stiff as he dried his hands. Maybe he wasn't interested in her physically.

"I'm excited to try my turn with that ax. You made it look easy," she said as they sat down.

The steam was still coming off the eggs, but he dug in. After taking several bites, he followed it with a long drink of water before meeting her eyes. She sensed a challenge.

"I may need to chop down a tree that looks a little shaky. Could be the one housing the coyote from last night."

She narrowed her eyes at him. "Coyotes don't live in trees. Besides, you'd never let them hurt me."

He harrumphed before digging back into his plate.

"How'd you learn to do all this, remodeling a cabin and scaring off coyotes?" She hoped she could keep up with him today.

"My dad and uncles were always doing something

around the cabin. I guess I just watched a lot. When my dad spotted this one for sale, I decided I needed another project."

"A special place to bring all your girlfriends?" she teased.

He set his fork down on his clean plate. "Nope, you're the first woman to visit the cabin."

His face softened, and her heart pounded.

"I'm honored."

"Breakfast was good. Where'd you learn to cook?" His guard was back up, but she'd seen a flash of vulnerability in that moment. Maybe he needed her to make the move, maybe he was unsure about crossing the line between protector and damsel in distress?

"My mom and grandmother insisted we learn. My sister is more of a baker, and I mastered the savory dishes."

"Lucky for me, I don't have much of a sweet tooth unless it's brownies."

"Noted. My grandmother always said there were two ways to a man's heart. His stomach is the second."

Grunting, he took a sip of his coffee. "Are you close with any of your father's family?"

Everyone knew her father came from an American dynasty of wealth and privilege. The Nash name was synonymous with success in many circles. But what people didn't know was her dad's family was all about appearances and focused on the family name, not the family.

"I don't remember a time my father's family was ever in the picture. He inherited the family fortune long after he made all his own wealth, so he's mostly self-made. His father rejected his business ideas and refused to invest in the early days, but most people assume it's all family money. I don't have many memories of my grandparents, but I always had the impression my paternal grandparents weren't very accepting of my mother."

"Family dynamics are always complicated in some way."

"Your family seems amazing, hard-working, loving, but maybe your parents created big shoes to fill?"

"Very perceptive. My folks and grandparents set the bar high, that's for sure. That's probably why Charlotte's the only one who's married yet."

"So you're just a gorgeous, protective man, looking for the right woman to bring home to Mom and Dad?"

His laughter filled the room, and his smile felt like a thousand rays of sunshine.

"When you put it like that, it sounds a little childish."

"Not at all. I could tell your parents are fantastic after meeting them for five minutes. It must feel like a lot of pressure to find someone that will fit in and measure up."

"I haven't honestly been looking. Too focused on work to try."

The space between them seemed small and vast at the same time. He was looking for all or nothing with someone, and the only examples of lasting love she had were from romance novels she indulged in once and a while.

"I'll clean up and put on some pants then meet you outside," she said, taking both their plates to the sink.

If she made a move, was it for the moment or could they try to be more? Would he even consider someone like her with laser focus on her career?

He made a beeline for the deck but paused after opening the sliding glass door as if he could read her thoughts. Rory

Maguire was a disciplined machine, but there was no way he didn't feel the constant hum of something between them. They weren't leaving this cabin until they both acknowledged there was something there. Now she needed to work up the confidence to make her move.

Chapter Eighteen

WATCHING AINSLEY BEND over, while hearing her grunts and heavy breathing before she stretched her arms up to the sky, was driving him mad. An hour into helping him with yard work, they both decided she was better suited to do yoga on the deck. Turning his back to her, he picked up the ax again to chop up the tree he'd cut down and let off some steam.

"I'm going to go try out that tub," she called just as he went to swing the ax again, causing him to miss the piece of wood he'd been aiming for.

Luckily, he just hit the stump instead.

He let his arms hang to his sides in defeat as he stared up to the sky, tempted to pray for self-control.

"I need to make sure the seal is good before you can use it. I installed it the last time I was here but didn't get a chance to test it out yet."

"Okay, I can just take a shower."

"No, no, it's as good a time as any to test it out."

When he looked up at her, she was bending over to roll up the towel she'd used as a yoga mat. Cursing, he walked past her into the house, kicked off his dirty boots, and made his way up the stairs to turn on the water for the tub. He was

99 percent sure it would be fine, but he didn't want to risk not checking. Now his controlling tendency to make sure he didn't damage the new upgrades was at war with his ability to resist being near Ainsley. After rinsing out the tub, he turned the knobs to let warm water fill the old brass basin. Squatting down he looked for any sign of a leak, but everything looked fine.

Thankfully, she was giving him space, and once the tub was a third of the way full, he decided to go downstairs and confirm there was no sign of trouble. Before he could exit the bathroom, she walked in with only a sports bra and her leggings on.

He stopped in his tracks as she pulled her hair out of the messy bundle on her head. Her dark locks cascaded over her shoulders. He could swear her eyes were darker, and he didn't miss the telltale sign of her nipples pebbling.

"Did you want to join me?" she said, walking closer to stop in front of him.

His mouth was dry.

"Is that a trick question?" he asked.

If this was her idea of a game, he didn't want to play. She had to know how desirable she was.

"No. I'm inviting you to stop being so serious. In fact, I'm daring you to tell me you're not feeling this electric vibe between us. Or to indulge in it."

"Of course, I feel it. I'd have to be dead not to feel it."

She gripped his shirt in her hands. "Then why aren't you acting on it? I've been trying to get your attention all morning."

"You've had my attention from the moment we met, but

I didn't think it was wise to mix business with pleasure."

"Our business ended." Reaching one hand up to his chest, she pulled his mouth down to hers. Her other hand snaked up under his shirt, and she was making it clear she wanted him just as much as he wanted her. He felt like he'd just won a marathon.

Gripping the back of her head as their kiss grew desperate, her lips opened to him. His other hand found its home on her ass as he pulled her against him. There was no denying how much he wanted her, and he was sick of ignoring it. She was offering him her body, but he couldn't help but want more. He wanted to possess her body, mind, and heart. The thought was shocking, but he couldn't deny it.

She pushed his shirt up, and their mouths separated for a second while he pulled it off. Picking her up, her legs wrapped around his hips while he walked out of the bathroom and lay her on the bed. Covering her with his body, he balanced his weight on one arm above her. She bucked her hips against him as her knees framed his waist.

He wanted to explore every curve of her, starting with the tender skin of her midriff exposed above her leggings. She was in phenomenal shape, but the softness of her skin was the real prize. He wanted to know if every inch of her felt this way.

"Rory." She whispered his name as a plea, and he didn't need any more encouragement.

Pulling her leggings down, he peeled them off her fast but took his time sliding his hands back up her muscular curves. Her supple skin begged to be stroked until a sound broke through the fog of lust he was feeling.

"Shit, the tub." He jumped off the bed and moved to the bathroom just in time to turn off the faucet. The water was on the precipice of cascading over the edge of the tub, and it gave him a split second to consider what they were about to do.

"Get back here, Sergeant, and that's an order," she called playfully.

Stepping back into the main room with his jeans unbuttoned and his chest heaving, he found her sprawled on the bed propped up on her elbows. One leg was angled up, and she moved it slowly back and forth as if she was enjoying a lazy afternoon.

"Please," she said, eyes full of desire.

"You're not in charge here," he said, moving to kneel in front of the bed and gripping her ankles.

He pulled her toward him so that the back of her knees could bend on the edge of the bed. Running his hand up her thighs and over her hips, he watched her excitement mix with need in her eyes. Her lips were parted, and her cheeks were rosy. Next, he gripped her panties before slowly sliding them down and kissing along their trail.

"Turns out, I like it way better when you're in charge," her strangled voice said as she watched him work.

"Emmm." He let his lips vibrate over her delicate skin before darting his tongue out to taste her. "I thought you might."

Looking into her eyes, he sunk his mouth over her and watched as her eyes closed and her head fell back against the bed. Then he increased the pressure with his tongue. She tried to lift her feet to give him better access, but he wanted her right where he had her. Gripping her thighs to stay lying flat against the side of the bed, while spreading them wider. He used his teeth to increase the intensity while his hands explored her curves. Her body began to convulse as she groaned his name and writhed beneath him. He reveled in the view. Her hands clenched the sheets, her neck arched back, and she was lost in his touch.

A few moments later, she called out his name as she shattered against his hand. He moved up her body, kissing her lush skin along the way.

"You taste as good as you look," he murmured.

"You feel as good as you look," she said through a laugh, "and that's saying a lot."

After letting her head lull back and forth a few times she looked down at him where he rested his chin between her breasts, still hidden under her skimpy sports bra.

"Do you have a condom?" she asked.

"Nope," he grunted.

"Not such a great prepper, are you?"

"I didn't plan for you."

"I can't believe there's never been a woman out at the lake that caught your attention." She sat back up on her elbows to study him.

"I spent most of my days off last year working on the remodel, and I haven't dated anyone serious enough for a weekend getaway."

"Why is that?" She ran her hand through his hair, and the feel of her fingers on his scalp was intimate.

"I've been concentrating on my career."

"You sure that's the only reason why?"

"I'm not one of your stories to puzzle out. Some men just don't want to settle down."

"Hmm." She wound her legs back up and circled his hips again before pushing him to lay next to her. Next, she rolled over to be on top of him before she leaned forward and started kissing his neck.

"Well, Mr. 'I'm too serious to let my guard down and have a real relationship,' I completely understand. I've been too focused on my career to worry about a happily-ever-after. I don't need any ties to make me second-guess myself." Her mouth pressed against his chest and then moved back up to his ear. "But in the meantime, we can have a little fun and put out this raging lust between us."

Sliding her hands down, she gripped his hard length in her hand.

"Now let's see what we can do to relieve some of the tension in your body."

He gripped her hips and relished the feel of her straddling him as she sat straight up. In one smooth motion, she pulled off her sports bra and threw it to the floor. Her hair fell just long enough to tease her already hard nipples.

"You're gorgeous," he said with a huskiness in his throat.

"So are you." She leaned back down, pressing her skin against his, and he rolled them back over so he was on top of her.

He captured one of her full breasts in his mouth, and she rewarded him by grinding her naked hips on him.

"Take off your pants," she ordered.

He almost laughed at her forceful command as he stood

and dropped his pants. Her naked form on his bed was enough to take his breath away.

"Hand me my leggings please?" Her voice was thick with lust.

Worried she changed her mind, he plucked her leggings off the floor and handed them to her.

At that moment, he was forced to admit to himself that he might be the kind of man who wanted something more than a casual affair. But she seemed content to let a physical connection between them play out. There was no need to complicate things.

He watched as she retrieved a plastic wrapper from a hidden pocket in the waistband of her leggings.

She held it up like a prize and smiled.

"You were prepared to seduce me?"

"Lucky for us, I'm a better prepper than you."

Kneeling between her legs on the bed, he leaned back over her, knowing she was going to have her way with him and smiled at the thought. She slowly unwrapped the condom, then rolled it down over him. It was sexy as hell, and he throbbed for her. She had all the power, and by the look in her eyes, she knew it.

"We'll need to run to the store tomorrow for more," she said, gripping his hips and pulling him toward her.

"You're the boss," he said.

It took all his strength to wait at the precipice of her core as she stroked him back and forth through her wet heat. Then she lifted her hips off the bed, slowly impaling herself with him before pulling him down over her. With excruciating patience, he hovered above her, and gave her time to adjust to his size.

"I want all of you," she begged beneath him.

Her hands gripped his back pulling him closer and he strained to resist taking what he needed. Her mouth was on his, and he could taste her passion.

"I don't want to crush you," he warned as he sunk deeper into her warmth and felt the rising tension.

"Crush me. I want you as close as possible," she said, hiking her knees up higher along his sides, and he sank even further.

Picking up the tempo her breath hitched and her hips met his in rhythm as both their bodies melded together.

Slowing down, he let the sensations settle over him for several breaths before he started driving deeper again, taking them both into an explosive release that was long overdue.

Chapter Nineteen

LISTENING TO RORY'S breath settle down felt intimate. Her own pounding heart began to return to its normal pace, but she couldn't help but worry about what this would mean between them. Rory was no longer her bodyguard. He was her lover. She needed to play it cool and not overanalyze how he'd known exactly what she needed or how their bodies fit together perfectly. Wanting to know him better was probably her inquisitive instinct and had nothing to do with the raging desire she'd developed for him since they'd met. Tracing the lines that carved out his well-defined abs as they lay in bed, she hoped she could keep her feelings separate from her desire for him.

"Should we try out the tub?" she suggested and felt his laugh through his chest where her head was laying.

He'd been running his fingers through her hair and letting it fall to her back, also lost in thought when she spoke.

"I better drain some of the water if we're both getting in."

"Okay, I'll watch." She sat up and ran her eyes over him, enjoying the chance to openly appreciate his easy gorgeousness. "You're too sexy for my own good."

"It didn't seem to be an issue last week. I must have

worn you down with my charm," he said.

His dimple was on full display, even through the several days' worth of scruff, and the left side of his mouth hitched up.

"You should smile more. That's what tipped the scales in your favor," she said, kissing his dimple.

"Oh, really." He sat up and ran his hand along her leg up to her breast before running his thumb back and forth over the tightening peak.

"The best decision I ever made," she whispered.

He trailed his hand up her neck into her hair and brought his mouth down over hers while pushing her back into the frumpled sheets. She was lost again in the desire he evoked. She could feel the wet heat pooling already between her legs. This time she pushed him back and straddled him without letting their lips separate.

"On second thought, I think I'd rather get a little dirtier before we bathe."

His smile was like a prize she won, and when his hands gripped her hips, she moaned with pure pleasure. He could have anything he wanted from her. All he had to do was ask. The possession she felt over him was a bad sign, but it wasn't going to discourage her from enjoying every naked minute with him.

His hand gripped the hair at the nape of her neck as he gently pulled her mouth down on his, and his other hand skimmed her hot skin along her back. Breaking their kiss, he stroked his tongue along her neck and teased her ear lobe.

Moving her hips along his length caused more friction between them that drove her head to arch back and her legs to twitch. His mouth captured hers again as his hands ran down her thighs then back up to knead into her curves, and she couldn't resist grinding over him.

"You're going to pay for that," he said before he flipped her onto her back, and the tension continued to build. This man might be the first to distract her from her goal of a national correspondence position, and it would be completely worth it.

An hour later after thoroughly enjoying his skills in bed, she woke up alone. "Rory," she called.

He appeared in the bathroom doorway, and she heard the water draining.

"No bath?"

"I was just adding more hot water. Get those lazy bones out of bed."

She walked naked from their bed into the bathroom and found the tub filled with bubbles. He had his jeans back on, but they were slung low, giving her a glimpse of his muscular, round butt as he bent over the tub to turn off the steaming water. After dipping his hand into the suds, he stood back up.

"You would have made a great plumber. Women would have constantly broken pipes."

Laughing, he reached out to her and captured her smile in a kiss as if it were normal for them to kiss all the time. She wondered if it could be.

"The water should be perfect," he said.

She noticed a slight blush and found his bashfulness endearing. Closing the space between them, she wrapped her arms around his waist and smiled. Normally, she would feel a bit more self-conscious strutting around naked, but the way he'd touched her and practically worshiped her in bed gave her more confidence.

Leaning down, he kissed her upturned mouth, and she was tempted to drag him back to bed. Patting her naked bottom, he ended the kiss before she could get too lost in the emotions swirling.

"Get in the bath, and then we'll go for a drive for a few amenities."

She laughed knowing he meant condoms in bulk.

"I'll be right back. I'm going to grab us a glass of water."

Not one minute in the tub, and her phone began ringing. But then she remembered she had turned it off. It must have been Rory's phone. She hadn't heard him come back up the stairs. Was something wrong? Unable to relax in the warm suds, she begrudgingly pulled herself from the tub. She could hear him talking to someone as his voice floated up the stairs. After wrapping herself in a towel, she walked out of the master bedroom onto the landing.

"Yes, I understand this is an amazing opportunity. I'll tell her you called." He sounded annoyed, and she heard him huff before his feet padded toward the stairs.

He looked up to find her eavesdropping.

"New York called. They want you for some audition tomorrow." He had a forced smile, but she could see the disappointment in his eyes. He walked up the steps and handed her a cool glass of water.

"Your producer is resourceful. Said your phone was off, so he did some kind of web search for my contact information."

She laughed at his surprise. "Reporters are proficient at online stalking."

"I guess so. He said you need to call him back to confirm the details."

He walked past her into his bedroom and grabbed his t-shirt off the floor where one of them had discarded it. Then she watched as he gathered a few new items from the dresser. Digging her phone out of her things, she powered it on and found fifteen missed calls and texts from her producer. The last one read: *Audition is at noon tomorrow in studio three in New York. You can't pass this opportunity up for a fling. Call me.*

Heaving a sigh, she sat on the bed, avoiding his gaze. He stood less than five feet away, but it may as well have been a mile. The distance between them started growing the second the outside world intruded again.

"This story is my big break into prime time."

"I know. I just need to take a quick shower, lock up, and we can be on the road."

When she looked up, he'd already turned away to walk into the bathroom. He closed the door, and a minute later the shower turned on. Her entire body screamed to join him, but she knew it would just cost her more time, and she needed to get back to the city, pack, rehearse pitch material, book a train to New York, and get there before noon tomorrow.

Having already rinsed off in the tub, she opted to get herself dressed and pack up all her things, which she managed to do fast so she could avoid the temptation of seeing Rory in nothing but a towel. Grabbing her bag, she hauled it downstairs just as she heard him turn off the shower. She tidied up the kitchen and stood to look at the lake again while waiting for him.

His crisp scent wafted down the stairs, and she heard him gather his things. Finally facing him, she recognized the tension in his shoulders. It had been there when they first met. His features were schooled to a formality that he must use to protect himself.

"I'm sorry our trip was cut short, but I hope we can resume getting to know each other when I get back from New York," she said.

The minute she said it, she knew it sounded detached. She walked closer to eliminate some of the awkwardness between them, but he didn't open his arms to her. Sliding her hand into his, she tried to push past his cold demeanor. She realized maybe it wasn't disappointment she'd seen but indifference. Maybe this was how it was always going to be once they left the cabin. A fun, sexy, fling for a few days, then back to strangers.

"I just need to clean out the fridge, take out the trash, and turn off the water. I probably won't get back out here again until summer," he said, pulling his hand from hers to open up the fridge.

Five minutes later, she stood outside in the front drive, catching the first hints of the sunset as it cast the cabin in an orange glow. Rory exited the front door and locked it up.

"Let's go," he hollered as he walked to his SUV.

Before he got in the driver's side, she caught him and pulled his hand toward her. He didn't resist and turned to face her. Stepping up on her tiptoes, her mouth found his in a passionate kiss. He ran his hand up to her neck while she poured all her emotions into their lips pressed together. When she could feel the stirrings of something more than sexual need, she broke the kiss.

"Thank you for bringing me here," she whispered.

Chapter Twenty

ONCE HE WAS home, Rory realized how exhausted he was from all the cabin chores and sex. It was hard to believe just a few hours ago he was enjoying Ainsley's moans of pleasure, and now he was alone in his quiet living room, forced to take stock of everything that had happened since he met her. He'd been out of the office for a week but didn't miss the team. He wasn't sure if that was good or bad. Law enforcement was his passion, his life. Shouldn't he be itching to get back to work? Picking up his phone, he called the squad room, unsure who was on shift that day.

"Jake, hey, I wanted to let you know I'll be in tomorrow for the day shift. You can put me back on the rotation and take a few days off."

Jake had been covering his sergeant shifts with longer shifts.

"I thought you were taking the entire week off. You sure you don't need a day to decompress?"

"Nah, I'd come in tonight if I thought I could stay awake. I just need one more good night's sleep."

"Alright, I'll see you at roll call tomorrow."

"Sounds good. See you then." After hanging up, he punished himself in the home gym, ordered takeout, and crashed. No call or text from Ainsley, but part of him didn't expect to hear from her. If he were honest with himself, he'd hoped she'd call him the second he dropped her off, but she didn't seem to be as affected by their connection as he was. Which was comical, considering he didn't do attachments.

If she was going to follow through on her dream to land a position in New York as a national news anchor, a fling with him wasn't going to get in her way. Not that he would want to. Maybe the reason he wanted her more was because she wasn't clingy.

The next morning, he woke to the sound of his alarm chiming. Grabbing his phone off the nightstand, he realized he'd slept so hard he missed several text messages. Three from his mom, checking in, and one from Ainsley. He clicked on Ainsley's name first.

Headed to New York on the morning train. Call me when you wake up.

Rory smiled at the message but stopped himself before calling her. What was the point? He didn't want anything serious, and she didn't need any distractions. She was headed to New York for an interview for her dream job. He didn't want to confuse either of them. Instead of calling her, he waited until he was ready for work and texted her a quick response.

I'm headed into work. Good luck today. They'd be fools not to offer you the job on the spot. In a moment of weakness, he included, *Let's celebrate when you get back.*

Maybe they could have one last hoorah before she moved to New York, no strings attached.

The three little dots floated over his phone but then

nothing.

He wondered if she didn't want to celebrate with him or was unsure how to break the news to him if they'd already offered her the job. He wondered if she would even come back.

✕

NO MATTER HOW long his shifts were, he couldn't escape Ainsley. Her story and her face were on every news channel. Even now at five a.m. as he stepped into the squad room after a particularly grueling takedown, there she was. The national network was playing teasers of her original story and her new feature as their political expert. She was their guest correspondent all week as they dug into the details of the latest political scandal to rock the nation. With the arrest of her father's chief of staff, several other senators were indicted. Senator Nash put out a statement that he wouldn't seek re-election unless the people of New York wanted him to. As Rory stood watching the screen, the weight of his gear felt heavier than usual. He never should have taken so much time away. It only made it more difficult to get back into the routine.

He and Ainsley had exchanged a few texts since she went to New York three days earlier, but they were both busy. He was working long shifts, and the stress of running the SWAT team had already seeped back into his bones. The responsibility for making sure his men made it home alive every day was heavy. He knew what happened when they were unprepared or he lost his focus. People could die. Ever since losing his best friend and brother-in-law, he vowed to never let something like that happen again.

"You look like hell," Jake said, breaking through his thoughts.

Sitting on the long bench in front of his locker, he huffed.

"Good thing this isn't a beauty contest."

He began pulling off the Velcro that secured the police patches on his SWAT vest. Removing the gear was always a relief.

"If you need more time to adjust your sleep schedule for the midnight shift, all you have to do is ask." Jake sat next to him.

"Nah, I think I'm good. Taking so much time away from the team just reset my clock."

"Sorry to add on, but Captain wants to see you," Jake said.

"Great."

He still needed to write up his report, and every minute longer it took there was one minute of sleep lost. Making his way through the precinct to the captain's office, he regretted not showering first. The smell of freshly brewed coffee lingered in the air, and several officials stopped to greet him. Even when your dad was retired, people knew who you were, especially since his dad was one of the best police commissioners anyone could remember.

Knocking on Captain Sullivan's door felt like going to the principal's office. Technically he had until tomorrow to tell her he wasn't taking the job at training, but there was no point in delaying it.

"Enter," she called out, and he let himself in.

"Obviously, I know you've made your decision, and it's not what I want to hear," Captain Sullivan said.

"I'm sure you have a list of more qualified officers that are ready for the next phase. I'm just not ready to give up the team," he said, knowing that wasn't the main reason he was turning down the job.

"I can understand that. I honestly didn't expect you to consider the job this long. Just one piece of advice, Rory, if I may."

"Of course." He leaned forward in his seat, trying not to squint his eyes from the exhaustion he felt.

"One of my senior officers once said, always leave an assignment for your next job, not wanting to go."

He nodded because he knew who would give her that kind of advice. "My old man would say something like that."

She laughed. "And he'd be right. If you change your mind, let me know."

"It's good advice, I'm sure, and the job sounds great. I'm just not ready." He stood again and thanked her before heading back to the SWAT team building. It was his penance to stay there and try to make sure no other officer lost his life after Sam died, and so far, he had succeeded. It didn't seem fair for him to get to move on to a cushy job when Sam didn't even get to live to see his thirtieth birthday.

Chapter Twenty-One

D IGGING IN HER purse, she found her favorite lipstick and put on a coat of the shimmery pink shade before giving her hair a fluff. Makeup was like war paint for women sometimes, and she was ready for a battle.

Slamming her car door, she stomped her booties on the sidewalk as she approached the special team's doorway at the D.C. Metro Police Headquarters building. One of the officers recognized her and smiled broadly while holding the door open for her. Unsure if she was headed in the right direction, she walked down a hallway covered with an American flag, and police patches from all over. The hallway opened up into a large room with benches and lockers, and at the back was a desk where Rory sat. She enjoyed the look of surprise on his face for a split second as she walked up to him.

"Are you blowing me off?" she said, not caring how many of his colleagues could hear her. She was tired of playing phone tag with him, and she wasn't one to wait for answers.

He stood from his desk where he had been hunched over a laptop, his large hands making it look like a toy as he typed out something. He looked exhausted and sexy at the same time.

"Hello, Ainsley. Are you asking for an official statement, or is this a social call?"

His attempt at sarcasm felt like a warning of how unwelcome she was.

"Let's call it personal curiosity." She crossed her arms over her chest. "What is going on?"

He walked around from behind his desk and gently placed his hand on the small of her back. Instant heat pooled in her belly, and shivers ran over her arms. Luckily, her long-sleeved blouse hid her reaction.

"Let's see if we can find some privacy to talk," he said by way of an explanation as he guided her toward what looked like a weight room behind glass windows. The room was empty, and he closed the door behind him.

She wanted to reach up and pull his mouth down to meet hers, but she hesitated. His smile was forced, and his eyes watched her as if she was a stranger.

"Hi," was all she managed.

"Hi, how is your new job?"

"I'm not sure yet. I'm still waiting for an official offer. They're sorta testing me out to see how I mesh with the New York crew."

"I've seen a few of your shows. You seem to mesh just fine," he said, but his smile didn't reach his eyes.

"You look like you're working too much."

"We've had a busy week."

"By busy, you mean violent."

"Yes, that's my job. We deal with the worst of the worst."

She closed the space between them and ran her hand up to his chest in an attempt to soothe the frustration she could see in his eyes. All her annoyance disappeared.

"I've missed you," she said, but wanting to say more.

His mouth was on hers before she could say anything else, and he walked her back against a wall out of view of the doorway. His hands were needy on her hips pulling her closer. She craned her neck back against the padded wall as his tongue delved beyond her lips. He was forceful, and she wanted him to rip off her clothes if it meant she could be closer to him. She wanted to feel his taut muscles and warm skin all over hers.

"Please tell me what you're thinking," she asked when his mouth moved over her ear.

His breath was hot on her neck as he gulped for air, and his hands stopped roving over her body.

"We can't do this here."

She wound her hands around his neck not wanting to let him pull away and held him closer.

"No, tell me what you're thinking about us. Obviously, you're still attracted to me, but why haven't you called me?"

Right on cue, his phone in his pocket began to chime and vibrate. They were still pressed close together, but she could feel him pulling back.

"Tell me?" she said looking into his hooded eyes.

"I'm back on the night shift and trying to get into the flow of long shifts and facing off with scumbags most nights. Today has already been a twelve-hour shift, and I'm on again tonight. You've been in New York, testing out for your dream job. We're moving in different directions. I didn't think there was anything else to discuss."

Like the weightlessness you feel on an airplane when there is bad turbulence, her stomach dropped.

He didn't want her.

"Nothing else to discuss?" she repeated.

His phone continued to ring, and she heard a phone out in the squad room begin to buzz.

"So you want me to believe this thing between us was just an overwhelming physical connection that means nothing more?"

He stepped back and pulled his phone from his pocket as it continued to ring. She looked up into his eyes, and they were guarded.

"The truth is, I'm not capable of anything more. This job doesn't leave room for more. Your move to New York only solidifies the fact that it was never going to work."

The sting of tears made her madder than his bullshit response.

"Okay, Sergeant. Thank you for clearing that up for me. I'm sorry I wasted your time today."

Opening the door, she walked out. He didn't try to stop her, no goodbye, nothing. Forcing a smile against the swell of emotion in her throat, she didn't let a tear fall until she was back in her car. She didn't know what she had expected. It wasn't like he was going to see her and suddenly profess his love or beg her not to go to New York. Rory Maguire was a stoic, wounded man and had even warned her he wasn't interested in anything remotely like a relationship. She wasn't interested in a relationship either, or at least she hadn't been until she met him.

Clearing the air with him should make her decision to leave D.C. easy. It was a clean break. If she was offered the job in New York, she had nothing holding her back.

Only, somehow, in the last ten years while chasing a national news correspondent position, she forgot to take stock and see if her dream had changed. She was turning thirty this year and hadn't had a serious relationship since college. Did she want one? She'd thought her dad was the enemy, and now she realized he was her favorite parent. If she stayed in D.C., they could get to know each other again and start over. But what did she want?

For now, she was in D.C. until the network decided if they wanted to offer her the correspondent job in New York, but she needed to know what her answer would be.

Instead of driving home, she found herself parked outside her dad's row house near the Capitol. She didn't even know if he was home but decided she wasn't ready to go back to her empty condo to be alone. Her dad answered the door before she had a chance to knock.

"There's my little star," he said, holding his arms open at the top step.

Walking up each step, the tears started to blur her vision.

"You used to call me that when I was a kid, and I thought I was going to be an actress when I grew up."

After a tight squeeze, her dad ushered her inside to his cozy study where the gas fireplace just reminded her of Rory's cabin.

"What's wrong?" her dad asked, setting a box of tissues next to her. He leaned forward across from her and held her hands.

"I'm not sure what I want anymore."

"Is this about work, love, or both?"

Laughter bubbled up her chest. "What's love got to do with it?" she said, looking into the fire.

"Well, it seems to me, you and the dashing sergeant developed a strong connection."

"I thought so, but it appears I was wrong." She met her dad's eyes. "But even if we had, I couldn't pass up my dream job for a relationship. Right?"

Her dad shrugged. "Why not? Is it a real dream job if it takes you away from someone you could see a future with?"

"You're confusing me more. I thought you would say always put your dreams first."

"Now that sounds more like something your mother might say. I'm not saying there isn't a time in your life you need to focus solely on yourself and your dreams. I think the real question is do you still want to be the correspondent in New York, or did you outgrow that dream? You're very good with political reporting. What about being one of the White House correspondents or on the Hill? Aren't those just as prestigious?"

"I suppose they are. Which means they're very competitive. The hours can be grueling but probably no more grueling than New York."

"It would seem to me you have a lot of bargaining room right now. Which is worth nothing if you're not sure what you want."

Rubbing her head, she wondered if either of those positions were even available.

"Remove your relationship with Rory from the equation

and think about which city you love more. Where do you want to build your home? Because whichever move you make, that will be your home for the foreseeable future. So where do you see yourself? Do you want to get married in the next five years? Maybe have a few kids?"

Her dad posed the questions in his soothing voice, and she considered all the variables.

She wanted to laugh but her stomach clenched as she pictured a baby with green eyes, a dimple, and wild tawny hair.

"I've only ever thought it would be New York, but being there for the last week, I felt like a tourist. Even after growing up there, it didn't feel like home anymore. Maybe because you and Mom and Amelia aren't there?"

"I still have an apartment in the city. You're welcome to have it. And I can start traveling back to New York again when we're not in session. We can still spend more time together if you take the job there. Your mom and sister live there most of the year, so you'll see us all the time."

"That's true." She squeezed her dad's hand. "So I just need to decide if I want the dream I've been chasing or a new one."

"I know what will help. A big scoop of ice cream. You should always make serious decisions over dessert."

✖

THE NEXT DAY, before she finished the evening news segment, the network surprised her by connecting her with the New York nightly news show. Live on air, they offered her the job she always dreamed of taking. There was confetti and splashy graphics behind her on the screen, welcoming her to the New York team. After they went off the air, the producer in New York called to formally offer her the job.

Somehow it felt anticlimactic, like she was missing something or leaving the house without her keys. She couldn't put her finger on why it didn't feel one hundred percent right. Maybe it was the culmination of finally achieving something and leaving her life in D.C. behind. Even after talking to her dad about it, she didn't know what she was going to do until that exact moment when it became crystal clear.

Chapter Twenty-Two

EVER SINCE LEAVING the cabin and seeing Ainsley, Rory had been in a foul mood, but not bad enough to miss her evening news segment. Even though he needed the extra three hours of sleep before his next shift, he set his alarm in time to see her six o'clock report. When the camera focused on her, he could barely blink. Her dark hair was down in big waves, and her eyes sparkled. Polished, poised, and gorgeous. It was poetic justice that he would have to watch her get the call on live television for the job that would take her away for good. She looked stunned as the confetti fell around her, and everyone congratulated her. That was the last image he saw before the network rolled to commercials.

He planned to try to get in another few hours of sleep but only tossed and turned, so instead, he did a brutal workout. On his drive to the office, his phone started blowing up with calls and texts. When he realized the missed calls were from his dad and his brothers, he phoned Conner back.

"What happened?" he asked.

"Mom was in a car accident. She's at Mercy Hospital. I'm on my way now," Conner said. "Meet me there."

Putting his truck back in the drive, he flipped on his police lights and peeled out of the parking lot.

"I'll see you there," he said before hanging up. The three-mile drive to the local hospital was a blur.

As a cop, he was unfortunately quite familiar with the Mercy Hospital. After leaving his truck parked out front, he easily found his brother in the emergency room. Conner had just gotten the details and intercepted him.

"Mom's in surgery. Dad and Finn are in a family waiting room."

"How bad is it, and what the hell happened?" Rory said, letting his fear show.

"The nurse said she was conscious when she came in, but her leg was injured in the crash. Her car was totaled."

He felt a wave of relief knowing his mom had been conscious, but they both knew things could go south with internal bleeding and any myriad of complications.

"Alright, let's go find them." Pushing past his brother, they made their way through the crowded halls to the family waiting room. His dad was hunched over with his elbows on his knees, and Finn sat grim-faced while rubbing their dad's back. Although they were an affectionate family, it wasn't common for him to see his former Navy SEAL brother looking so vulnerable.

"What happened?" He couldn't help his accusatory tone.

It was ten o'clock. Why was his mom even out driving so late alone?

His dad's weary eyes met his, and he was struck by how much older his father suddenly looked. He'd been crying, which was a really bad sign. Finn stood.

"Mom's car was t-boned by some kids out joyriding. Her

leg is broken in three places. The doctor is putting in a rod and pins or something, but it may not take. A portion of her bone was crushed. She's going to be in a lot of pain and may need a second surgery," Finn said.

"Why was she even out so late?" Rory demanded.

"Your mother ran out to the grocery store around nine. She said she needed a few things for the dinner party she planned this weekend. Usually, I'd go with her, but I was busy fiddling with the new lights she wanted on the deck.

"Dad, it's not your fault," Finn said with an eerily calm tone.

"You shouldn't have let her go at all," Rory said.

Finn's eyes narrowed on him, and Conner gripped his elbow.

"Don't you dare. It's not Dad's fault some little shits were speeding in a stolen car and hit Mom. If Dad had been with her, she could have died. The passenger side was demolished," Finn said.

His stomach rolled, and his anger ebbed. Finn was right, but his fear took over and he lashed out. It was just like when his best friend was shot. He was helpless and at the mercy of the doctors and fate. He hated that feeling.

Conner pulled him away and walked him toward a window.

"You have to stop acting like you can control everything in life. Bad shit happens no matter how careful and regimented you are," Conner said.

His throat constricted, and he couldn't speak beyond the emotions that threatened to swallow him up. A moment later, he felt his dad's hand on his back.

"She's going to be fine, Rory. We just need to pray and trust the doctors know best." His dad enveloped him in a hug. As hard as he fought it, his eyes clouded, and his vision blurred.

"It's not the same as when we lost Sam. I spoke to your mom before surgery. She was chatty once the painkillers kicked in. She'll be bossing us all around for months to come while she heals up."

Before he could respond, a few more officers entered the family suite along with some of their mom's colleagues. As a prominent judge in the city, her position was demanding and prestigious within the community. Word would spread quickly that Cora Maguire was hurt, and the hospital would be a zoo.

Finn intercepted everyone while he and his dad collected themselves.

"I'm sorry, Dad," Rory said, choking back emotions.

"It's fine, son. It's not a bad thing that your knee-jerk reaction is to be protective. It's in your nature."

"Maybe to a fault," Rory admitted.

"You can channel it by helping me convince your mom she'll have to cancel her party and take time off of work." His dad gave him a final squeeze.

Rory laughed. His dad was not exaggerating. His mom wasn't the type of woman to sit back and relax.

Soon after Finn got rid of their mom's colleagues, the doctors came back in to let them know the surgery was a success, and they could each take turns seeing her. Their dad went back first, and Rory sat between his brothers, feeling uneasy. Every aspect of his life seemed to be in upheaval. He couldn't get his bearings.

"I heard you turned down the job at the training center," Conner said by way of conversation.

"How the hell did you hear that?" Rory asked.

"Come on, I'm undercover. I know everything."

"Dad must have told you," Rory guessed.

Conner just shrugged. "I would've jumped at the offer if the captain had asked me. The program needs a reboot."

"I enjoyed running the underwater training for recruits in the Navy. It was rewarding but also a great reminder of how important our fundamental training was," Finn said.

"So you're both in favor of me going out to pasture and not doing real police work anymore?"

"Yes," they both said in unison.

"Damn, maybe I should call Charlotte to get more unsolicited career advice."

"Ya sure, but she'll just say you're long overdue for a break from the streets. You're going to burn out," Conner said casually as he stood.

Their dad appeared with a smile. "Your mom is still asleep. The doctor says it'll take another hour for the pain meds to wear off." He looked at his watch. "It's late. I'm going to sleep here tonight, but I know your mom will want to see you all when she wakes up."

"I'll run back to your place and pack you and mom a few things," Finn said, standing.

"I'll go with you," Conner said. "Rory, you stay here in case Dad needs something until we get back."

"Okay. While you're giving out orders, why don't you just run my life for me, Connie," Rory said, sitting back down, feeling annoyed his brothers thought they knew better.

"If that were the case, you'd be groveling at Ainsley Nash's feet and taking the job at training," Conner said before walking away.

"Sounds like a good plan to me." Their dad said as he sat next to him.

Rory stewed as he watched his younger brothers leave.

"Talk to me. What's going on in that stubborn mind of yours?" his dad asked.

"I turned down the offer to be the next director of training," he said and waited for his dad's reaction, but his old man just nodded.

"You never took a break or went out to training," Rory said.

His dad laughed.

"Because it's not a break. You'll be charged with making sure every recruit has all the training and skills they need to serve the community. Not to mention fire the ones who fall short. And then there are the officers already on the job who will be sent out for remedial training and the repeat offenders. You'll make a few enemies when you start to see people not taking their training as seriously as you do."

Rory mulled this over.

"I think you should take the job, but it doesn't matter much what your brothers or I think. What do you want? Are you happy with the grueling schedule on SWAT, or are you ready for a new challenge?"

"I'm starting to think I'm past due for a change."

"Well, I'd be remiss not to remind you that your mother

and I aren't getting any younger, and we sure would love some grandbabies who live closer to us."

"Dad, I'm nowhere near giving you grandkids."

"Not if you stay on the SWAT team, but maybe you should consider groveling at Ms. Nash's feet like Conner said." His dad chuckled as he stood. "I'm going back to be next to your mom in case she wakes up. I don't want her to be alone."

"Good night, Dad. I love you. Just text me if you need anything. One of us will be here all night." He stood and hugged his dad.

"I love you too, son. Think about where you see yourself in five or ten years. Then think about who is missing from your life in that scene." His dad gave him a knowing look.

The first person to pop into his mind was Ainsley, but there was no way to make that work living in different states. It wouldn't be fair to her if he begged her not to take her dream job, and he had no reason to think it would work even if she stayed.

After checking in with the office, he confirmed they had the team covered for his shift. Then he decided to camp out in the hospital waiting room until his brothers came back to relieve him. He must have fallen asleep, because the next thing he knew, Ainsley stood over him, shaking his arm. Her dark locks hung above him, and she smelled like coconut and sugar.

"Rory, I heard about your mom. I came to see if you need anything." she said in a hushed voice.

"Are you here, or is this a dream?"

Her smile pushed her high cheekbones out, and her eyes

glimmered.

She was wearing a fuzzy white sweater and held a tray of coffees standing within arm's reach.

"You look like an angel."

She laughed and held out a coffee for him.

Sitting up, he remembered crashing on the hard loveseat and instantly regretted it as his back stiffened. Sliding into an upright position, he ran his hand through his hair, knowing it was wild. Reaching out, he accepted the coffee and took a big gulp.

"Thank you for coming," he said, trying to shake the fog of sleep away.

She sat in the row of chairs across from him.

"How is your mom? Can I get you or your folks some breakfast?"

He studied her. She looked relaxed in yoga pants, and sneakers. His watch said six a.m.

"Why are you up so early?"

"I had my alarm set for yoga, but then I saw the story about your mom. So I came here. They think they caught the kids that hit her car."

He nodded, absorbing the information.

"I was rude to you, and you still came to check on me?"

"Well, your mom was so welcoming and lovely when I met her. I figured you'd be better equipped to help her and your dad if you had your morning coffee."

A smile pulled at her mouth, and he ached with a need he never experienced before meeting her.

Not wanting to say the wrong thing, he sipped his coffee and stared. What was he supposed to do about her?

Before either of them spoke, Conner and Finn walked in looking bright-eyed and well-rested.

"Oh, good morning, Ms. Nash," Conner said.

Ainsley stood, and Conner gave her a quick hug by way of greeting, then introduced her to Finn. He couldn't decide if he was pissed or pleased that she felt so comfortable with his family.

"You brought Mom's favorite coffee? What a sweetheart," Conner said, plucking the cup out of Rory's hand and taking a big gulp. Next, Conner accepted the tray of coffees from Ainsley and offered one to Finn. "I'm going to go relieve Dad and see Mom," Conner said, waltzing out as if he were in charge.

"Here, you look like you need this more than me," Ainsley said, handing her coffee to Rory.

He was too dumbfounded to refuse, and then his dad walked through the door with a warm greeting.

"Ainsley, it's lovely to see you. Thank you for the coffee. Cora was ecstatic to have the delicious brew over the hospital swill." His dad then enveloped Ainsley in another big hug.

"I'm so glad she's well enough to enjoy it. Is there anything else I can bring to either of you?" Ainsley asked.

"Oh no, but we appreciate you dropping everything to check on us. Congratulations on your new job. Very impressive."

Rory imagined this was how it would feel if he and Ainsley were a real couple, and she attended all his family events with him or responded during emergencies. If she were his girlfriend, she would automatically be enveloped in the Maguire family.

"Dad." His sister, Charlotte, burst through the door and hurtled toward their dad. "How is Mom?"

Not more than a step behind her was her husband, Caleb, carrying a large purse and bag of New York-style bagels.

Rory finally stood but felt like a spectator in his own life. Watching as his family exchanged greetings, Finn introduced Ainsley, and his dad gave the update on his mom. The only person who looked slightly more uncomfortable than him was Ainsley. She walked back over to his side, and her hand landed on his forearm briefly before her hand fell away. With just a split second of contact, his skin felt a jolt of electricity like a shock, and his heart pounded.

"I'm going to get out of the way. Are you sure you don't need anything?" she asked.

"I'd walk you out, but I haven't gotten to see my mom yet," he said.

"No, I understand. See your mom and get some rest." She smiled before floating out of the room as if she had never been there.

"You sure do know how to blow perfectly good opportunities, don't you?" Conner said, taking his second cup of coffee.

"Damn it, stop stealing my coffee and taking shots at me. Who is with Mom?"

"Charlotte went when you were busy messing up what could be your last chance with Ainsley," Conner said.

Rory sat back down and stared after the exit, wishing he'd walked Ainsley out, even though he had no idea what he wanted to say to her or how to say it.

Chapter Twenty-Three

AINSLEY STEWED AS she pulled the delicate yellow-hued glassware with fading gold rims from her kitchen cabinet. To anyone else they were old champagne flutes, but to her, they were priceless heirlooms from her great grandmother. Every glass needed to be wrapped before being placed in the individual padded holes. She could hire someone to do it, but it seemed weird to have strangers touch all of her things and it kept her busy. She didn't need to move out of her place on a set date, but she didn't want to drag it out either.

One of the major perks of negotiating her new job as the D.C. political correspondent for her network's New York station was that she didn't have to move. But her dad owned several brownstones near his, which would also be closer to work. When he admitted he bought them hoping his girls would use them, she decided to try it out and see how they got along. The home was furnished, but she needed her personal items, clothes, and everything for the kitchen.

She had the next two days off before her new job started on Friday, which gave her plenty of time to pack things up and think about Rory. He was out of sorts when she found him passed out that morning at the hospital. She'd been so nervous to see him again but compelled to check on him. Part of her expected him to reject her and dismiss her concern, but then he called her an angel and looked at her with such desire. In his sleepy daze, he'd shown her raw emotion before turning back into his standoffish self.

A knock at her door brought her back to the moment, and she wondered if the new doorman in her building thought he had to deliver the pizza she ordered to her door. Usually, a resident popped downstairs to collect any food deliveries. Looking through the peephole, she was surprised to see the man dominating her thoughts, and she whipped open the door.

"Hi, I didn't know you offered a delivery service."

Rory stood with her pizza and a large bouquet of white flowers.

"Only on Tuesdays." His smile was shrouded in several days' worth of scruff.

"In that case, please come in," she said, holding the door open for him.

"These are a peace offering," he said, holding out the flowers before stepping in.

"I didn't know we were at war."

She accepted the flowers and gave them a sniff before ushering him farther into her apartment.

"Have you already had dinner?" she asked.

"No, my body clock is messed up. Typically, I'd be having breakfast before the night shift."

"You're not working tonight?"

He shook his head but remained quiet while she busied herself with filling a vase with water for the flowers and getting them each a plate. Her heart was pounding so loud she wondered if he could hear it. She didn't want to get her hopes up, but it seemed odd for him to seek her out after he made it clear he didn't want a relationship with her.

"My captain ordered me to take another night off to catch up on sleep. My first instinct was to come to see you."

His voice sounded gruff with emotion, and when she met his eyes, she could see everything she was feeling in their green depths.

Without a second thought, she walked into him and stood on her tiptoes to reach his mouth. Her invitation was more than welcomed as his hands slid down her hips to cup her bottom. He leaned down to catch her mouth with his, and their bodies molded to each other. Winding her arms around his neck, he hoisted her legs up to straddle his hips. His scruff scratched her skin adding to the sensory explosion of having his firm hands holding her pressed against his hard muscles. Pushing one hand into his hair, she deepened their kiss. The guttural groan that hummed from his mouth made her smile. He wanted her. He missed her too.

"Condoms in the bedroom" was all she managed between kisses.

He nodded and walked down the hall, still holding her, but before they made it to her room, he pressed her against the wall in the hallway. The cool material against her back had her arching toward him. His hips pressed into hers, forcing her in place, and his hands pushed her breasts up to meet his mouth. Frustrated by the fabric of her shirt, he pulled it up and off. His hot tongue was on her skin as she pulled her bralette down.

"I don't think you're going to get much sleep tonight here," she said, grinding her hips against the bulge he pressed into her.

"That's fine," he said.

One of his palms gripped her jaw as he forced her to look into his eyes. He thrust his hips up to emphasize how much he needed her before he took his time placing soft kisses on the side of her mouth and along her cheek. His breath was hot on her ear. "I'd rather spend all night inside you than sleep," he said.

Holding onto his muscular shoulders, she could feel the frenzy of need building up in her body. His outspoken desire for her was enthralling. She wanted to show him how much she missed him.

Without another word, he carried her into her room, and they tumbled onto the bed. Rory's touch and taste overwhelmed and drove her need for him. Before she knew it, they were both naked covered in a sheen of sweat as they rediscovered how each other liked to be touched. Limbs tangled, hands explored.

To her great pleasure, Rory made it his mission to kiss every inch of her body before driving into her and claiming every moan he pushed out of her with his mouth. He took command of her body as he held one of her knees up against her side leaving no room for escape. She languished in the intensity as the swell of her orgasm ebbed, and with every touch he owned her, she was a goner. Lights exploded behind her eyelids as she rode the pleasure of his body all over hers. Having slowed his pace to hover over her and watch, she found him smiling when she opened her eyes.

"My turn." She pushed him to lay back.

"Ainsley." Her name was a strangled plea.

"Shhh, baby. I'm going to give you what you need."

Leaning forward, she kissed him, while at the same time, sinking down on top of him, filling herself with him. His fingers dug into her hips, and she pulled away from his mouth to watch him enjoy her. His head rocked back, and his abdomen flexed. He was holding back, but she wanted to control his release. When she lifted her hips away from him, his dark eyes opened and narrowed on her.

"You're beautiful," he said with a sly smile before he bucked up.

She crawled her hands up his chest, leaning forward to steal another kiss and felt her pleasure spike.

"Don't stop," he begged, and his eyes locked with hers as she continued the riding motion until they both exploded.

The next morning, after a night of very little sleep, she woke to the feel of Rory running the tip of his finger up and down her back. She was facing him with one hand slung over his side and one of his thighs in between her legs. The instant wet heat that pooled would be embarrassing if his swollen length wasn't pushing against her belly.

Without a word, he pushed her back into the mattress and settled between her thighs.

"Good morning beautiful," he whispered into her ear.

His voice was scratchy with sleep. She wound her arms around his shoulders and squeezed him before raising her hips.

Neither spoke again until they were a pile of exhausted sweaty bodies.

"I hope you don't need to be anywhere today because I'm going to make you my prisoner," Rory said into the pillow where he lay with his eyes closed.

Pulling up a sheet over his gorgeous, ripped body seemed like a crime, but her skin was cooled off and she didn't want him to catch a chill.

"I'm going to make us some breakfast. We forgot to eat last night."

He smiled. "I didn't forget," he said before he slipped back into sleep.

Chapter Twenty-Four

WAKING TO THE smell of French toast and bacon wasn't nearly as delicious as the sight of Ainsley wearing his t-shirt while bringing him a cup of coffee.

"What time is it?" he asked.

"Only nine. Are you ready for some breakfast?" she said as she walked back out of the room.

He sipped the hot coffee, wondering how this conversation was going to go. Would she be open to trying a long-distance relationship? Was he even capable of having a serious relationship? As much as he didn't know, he did know he wanted to try with her.

Out in the living room, he noticed the stacks of boxes against one wall. A pit in his stomach formed at the thought of her living in a different city and being so out of reach.

"Do you like whipped cream on your French toast?" she asked with a smile.

There was a large stack with all the fixings on two plates at the counter.

"No thanks." He sat down, knowing the food was going to taste like dust as annoyance settled over him.

Who was he kidding? Just because they had a sexual connection didn't mean they had any chance at a real relationship. He wasn't even capable of committing to a pet because his hours were so insane. How would he commit to a woman living in another city? A gorgeous woman with men hitting on her all the time.

A nudge from Ainsley broke through his thoughts.

"Eat up. You're going to need your energy after this." She leaned over his arm, offering up her mouth in a kiss.

The gesture was simple and carefree, but it only solidified how much he didn't want to try to force something that would only drive them both crazy. He kissed her soft lips before pulling away with regret.

Forcing a smile, he poured a stream of syrup on his plate and attempted to eat. It didn't help that Ainsley was moaning about how delicious every bite was.

"You sound like you're having a foodgasm," he said.

"Don't be jealous. I'll save my best moans for you," she said, poking him with her fork before digging back in.

He took another big gulp of his coffee to fortify himself.

"That's a lot of boxes packed up already. When's the big move?" He didn't face her, just stared off ahead, punishing himself with each gulp.

"Does it matter?"

Her tone was defensive and he knew she was still hurt by his previous rejection, but at the time, he didn't think he was capable of having more. He still wasn't convinced he should risk getting involved with someone while on the SWAT team. Even though he had turned it down, he was still mulling over the job at the training center. It would be a 180 in his career plans but would free up most of his weekends.

"Just because you brought me flowers, and we spent all

night exploring each other's bodies, doesn't mean I think you've changed your mind. I'm not that good. You were very clear when you said you don't have room in your life for someone like me."

Now he did face her. "No, I said I don't have room for a relationship, that my career doesn't exactly create an environment to foster a healthy relationship. It's not you, Ainsley. You're spectacular."

Her ire dimmed, but her smile didn't meet her eyes.

"How do you know if you've never tried?"

A glimmer of hope in her eyes felt like a sucker punch.

"Because I was there the night my brother-in-law was killed in a shootout, and I was the one who had to tell his wife, my sister, that he was dead."

Her eyes filled with tears and she reached out to comfort him, but he stood up and walked toward the sink with his plate and cup.

"The kind of work I do isn't good for relationships, but it's what I'm good at."

She nodded while swiping at her eyes and turning away from him. "I'm not going to try to change your mind."

In that moment, he knew what it meant to feel gutted. He'd fallen for her so fast, but they never stood a glimpse of a chance.

"At least we had last night and the lake cabin," she said, standing and taking the rest of her uneaten food to the sink.

She wasn't asking him to try to have more with her. She must know a long-distance relationship would just delay the inevitable. Or maybe she knew he wasn't the kind of guy she'd be willing to try to make a future with.

"I better go before this gets any more difficult," he said, backing up to give her space.

"Too late." She was in his arms in two strides and kissing him like they hadn't just broken each other's hearts.

Feeling her tears on the skin of his cheek as they kissed only turned the knife. He couldn't stand the lure of wanting to relive their night together and ended the kiss. Clutching her hands, he moved her back to create space between them. Her scent surrounded him.

"Good luck with your new job. You should be proud of yourself for chasing your dreams."

"It's funny how much dreams change as you chase them. We get tunnel vision thinking we know exactly what we want," she said.

Swiping at a tear that escaped her watery eyes, he stole one more kiss and then headed for the door.

"Bye, baby," he said with one last look back. He paused long enough to see her face crease with pain before walking out. He wasn't made for goodbyes.

It was too early to go to work and he knew he would be too restless to sleep, so he drove out of the city. An hour later as he approached the small lake town, he regretted his impulse to try and escape thoughts of Ainsley or his future. Pulling up to his cabin, he knew he would only see her if he went inside. After walking around the back of the property, he sat on the deck and let his dad's question play over in his mind. What did he want?

The last thing he ever remembered wanting was getting on the SWAT team. He and Sam had both had one-track minds after college. Get on the police force and then the

SWAT team. They'd been inseparable and made it. At the same time, Sam had started dating his sister, and they'd gotten married. But Rory had been married to his work, and then when Sam died, everything got too real. The violence, the life and death situations, the need for extensive training, and complete focus on the job. He'd taken the approach that if he was obsessive and meticulous with every element, then he would never lose another officer or friend. That he could out train and out prepare the bad guys, but in the years since they'd lost Sam, at least a dozen more officers had been shot. Dedicating his life to police work was a worthwhile endeavor. Protecting and serving his community and following in his father's footsteps was meaningful, but was it all he wanted?

Staring out at the lake for two hours didn't give him the answer, so he made his way home to work out and get ready for his next shift. If he could just get back into his routine, maybe he would figure it out.

THAT NIGHT, WATER dripped from his brow as he hunkered down against the back porch of an arguably condemned row house in the southeast neighborhood of D.C.. They were on one of the most dangerous blocks in the city, waiting for the crisis negotiator to give them the green light to raid a home. They had the specs on the layout of the home built in the forties, but there was no way of knowing what updates may have been made or furniture that could be in their way if they needed to breach the doors.

A man had phoned the police department a little after eleven when his son had showed up with a gun and his two kids he didn't have visitation to see. The young man was angry about a recent child support lien put on his bank account and was taking it out on his ex and his kids. The man that called was the grandfather but worried about his son's behavior and didn't want to risk his grandkids' safety. Rory could hear the kids crying inside, and the perpetrator yelling at them to shut up. It had been three hours, and everyone was getting weary.

"Look alive, team echo. I think things are going downhill fast," Jake's calm voice sounded over the earbud radio he wore.

He didn't need to check his gear or his sights. He was ready. Ace was on the ram for the back door, and Rory would enter first, followed by two more teammates. Another team of five would breach the front door at the same time. That created the possibility of putting fellow officers in danger, in each other's path if they needed to shoot, but it also created such a level of chaos for the perp that they often froze before they could think to fire a shot.

They all waited for the two words the negotiator needed to say that would signal the situation had reached the level of risk to the children and the grandfather's life.

"Have hope," sounded over the radio as the negotiator's signal.

"Echo goes," Jake said.

Ace used the large metal ram to splinter open the back door.

Within eight seconds, each team member breached the

doors, children screamed, and fellow officers barked orders for everyone to get down and show their hands. The rooms were better lit than outside, and they had the advantage of being able to see the young man's hands as his gun hung by his side.

"Police, drop your weapon. Police, drop your weapon," Jake ordered in a calm command.

The perp hesitated for a moment, then looked down at his chest and the multiple beads of red dots from the officers' aim points. He dropped his weapon to the floor before shoving his hands to the sky.

A small child hurtled herself at Rory, and he enveloped her before taking her out the door he'd just barreled through. His pulse pounded, and he knew his gear would be wet and harsh against the little girl's shivering form, but he doubted she cared.

"You're safe, you're safe. Your mom is just down the street," he whispered to the child as she clung to his neck.

His weapon was on a sling, and he let it dangle at his side as he trudged through the back alley lined with more cops. There was an armored police truck and ambulance waiting while dozens of neighbors watched with their cellphones out. The little girl's sobs broke his heart, but he also knew they'd lucked out tonight. There had been no bloodshed.

Like a tidal wave, the action grew with paramedics looking over both children and their mom being reunited with them. The father was arrested and hauled away, but not before several neighbors shouted exactly what they thought about him. The grandfather looked frail and despondent with grief. His grandkids were traumatized, and his son was going to jail.

"You did the right thing calling us, sir," Rory told him.

"He wasn't always so angry, you know. Life dealt him a few bad breaks, and he just dwells on all the bad things. Now he's going to lose his chance to see his kids grow up and enjoy the beautiful things in life," the grandfather said.

Rory didn't know what to say. It was highly likely the man was right. Best case, the young man got out on bail and got his life together, but the odds were, he would just find more trouble.

"There is always hope though, right?" Rory said.

The old man nodded before a paramedic escorted him to take a seat so she could check his vitals.

Holding the little girl, he'd had a vision of a mini version of Ainsley clinging to him. How could a parent ever let their child feel that kind of fear? Or worse, be the cause? He thought of how caring and warm Ainsley was. She would make an amazing mom. He'd always assumed he'd have his own family one day, but for some reason, hadn't given any thought to what it would entail to create one. The dedication to love someone enough to partner with them forever like his folks. The love needed to make choices that were for your family and not for yourself. Ainsley sat at the forefront of his mind, and he knew without a doubt he had messed things up with her.

After helping secure the man's doors that they'd bashed open in the raid, the team made their way back to the squad room to write up the report. Somewhere between hugging that little girl until she felt safe and finishing his report, Rory knew it was time for him to move on from the team. He needed more in life. He wanted more for himself and he needed Ainsley. Since it was only six a.m. the captain's office was empty and he made himself comfortable in one of the chairs facing her desk. He knew she'd be in soon, but he could rest his eyes while he waited.

"Maguire, I hope you're here looking like hell to tell me some good news," Captain Sullivan said, waking him up.

He popped up out of the seat and looked around to get his bearings.

"Captain, I'll take the position at training, if it's still available," he said.

"Sit down," she said, settling behind her desk.

"This is a five-year commitment, guaranteed to get you promoted to lieutenant."

"I'll take it," he reiterated.

"Weekends off, but you'll spend your days plotting new course work, researching new tools and techniques, planning class schedules, and documenting everything."

Rory nodded. "I'd like to start Monday to get a feel for how things have been running and get a grasp on what areas need the most improvement."

She nodded and a huge smile broke across her face. "Excellent. The job is yours, Maguire. I already had the chief sign off on it. Jake will take over the team."

"You knew I would take it?" He stood.

"I had a hunch. Why don't you tell Jake about his promotion before you go home and get some sleep? You really do look like shit."

"Thanks." He laughed and reached out to shake her hand.

"I'll keep this seat warm until you're ready for your next promotion," she said. "You're a born leader, Maguire, and you care. That's why I know you'll be great at training."

"We'll see," he said as he departed.

Once he was back in the squad room, it was quiet but for the steady sound of the morning news on a TV in the kitchenette. The shifts had changed over, but Jake was still there. He was probably waiting on him.

"So, what'd you decide?" Jake asked.

"You're looking at the new chief in charge of training, which makes you the new sergeant in charge of SWAT," Rory said, crossing his arms over his chest to mimic Jake's pose.

A huge smile broke out across Jake's face, and he stomped over to Rory, enveloping him in an awkward hug.

"I'm proud of you, man. You're moving forward again."

"What?"

Jake gave him a final slap on the back and took a step back.

"You've been like a hamster in a wheel, chasing your dad's legacy, while trying to live for you and Sam. You mastered this team years ago, and if you don't move forward, you'll be stuck the rest of your life."

"Are you dating some Zen master again or spending too much time with Father Flanagan?" Rory asked, running his hand through his wild hair.

"Don't hate."

"I'll come back tomorrow to clean out my desk and locker, but for now, I need to get some sleep."

"Maybe a shower too," Jake said laughing.

Grabbing his bag out of his locker, he was halfway to the exit when he caught sight of Ainsley on the TV.

Turning up the sound, he strained to focus on what she was saying. He didn't understand why she was standing on the front lawn of the White House instead of some sound stage in New York.

She looked vibrant in a magenta blazer with her hair piled up high. She was saying something about the latest scandal to hit the White House, and he wondered if he was hallucinating.

"I'll give you another update after the press secretary makes an official statement. Things are getting interesting at 1600 Pennsylvania this morning," Ainsley said with a sly smile.

The camera loved her. He loved her.

Then she was gone, and the picture changed to the correspondent in New York in front of Times Square. "Thanks, Ainsley, what a perfect first day as our D.C. correspondent."

"Thank you, Sara." The camera was back on Ainsley, and he was tempted to reach out to touch the screen. "I'm Ainsley Nash, bringing you a front-row seat to the latest political stories." She smiled before the camera panned away to the network's logo.

"Your girl got a promotion, huh?" Jake said, standing behind him with a fresh cup of coffee.

"She took the job in New York. I don't understand why she's still in D.C.."

"They just said she's the new White House correspondent. That's a pretty impressive gig. I bet they liked her coverage of that senate scandal. And she's obviously well-connected in this town."

Rory felt for his keys in his pocket and headed for the door as Jake blathered on. He didn't know what was going on, but he needed to find Ainsley and get some answers. The drive to the White House was short, but there was no parking anywhere near the actual street that ran in front of the national monument which also housed the first family on Pennsylvania Avenue. Luckily, his badge and cruiser garnered his entrance once the Secret Service verified his credentials. He pulled right in front of the police booth that the press used. He could still see Ainsley standing with the press pool on the famous pebble beach, which was just a small plot marked by gray stones where the press was allowed to broadcast their news segments.

"Ainsley," he yelled through the wrought iron fence just as the cameraman in front of her turned on a bright light.

She looked toward him, but a second later, she was lifting the microphone back up and talking into the camera. He watched and waited. Finally, she stepped away from the camera and walked down to the fence.

"Rory, is everything okay? You look exhausted." She stood within reach, but the fence was between them.

"I thought you were moving away," he said, pushing his face closer to the cold metal.

She looked back over her shoulder, and he noticed all the reporters were walking up the driveway. They must be headed to the press room.

"I moved into one of my dad's brownstones so I would have a better commute and be closer to him. We're working on our relationship."

"I thought you were moving to New York for your dream job?"

"Turns out, my dream job didn't fit my dreams anymore. I convinced the network to make me the new White House correspondent instead."

"You're not leaving?"

"No, but that doesn't change the fact that you don't want a relationship."

Before he could respond, the cameraman called her name.

"I have to go. It's my first day. I can't be late."

"Of course, um, I'll wait for you to get done."

"It's going to be a few hours, and you look beat." She started walking through the grass away from him.

"Call me when you're done, please," he called out.

She smiled and nodded before turning away to start jogging in her heels up the driveway. He didn't get a chance to tell her how amazing she looked or how he was an idiot.

Exhaustion had his body vibrating with fatigue as he drove out of the city to his place. As much as he needed a shower, sleep won out, and he passed out, fully dressed. He woke up curled up with his boots still on. The room was pitch black and the only sound was of the fan overhead rotating slowly in a circle. His mind was foggy as he recalled the long shift, the rain, the little girl who hugged him like he was her lifeline, and then Ainsley's face popped into his mind. She was still in D.C. He needed to tell her how he felt about her.

Conner had been right; he needed to grovel and pray he hadn't blown his last chance.

Digging his phone out of his pocket, it read seven o'clock. There were no missed calls. She was either swamped with work or had no intention of giving him a chance to grovel. Sitting up, he debated his next move. After getting a shower, he still had no grand ideas other than finding her and begging for a second chance.

Chapter Twenty-Five

WORKING THROUGH THE motions of downward dog, then back up into warrior pose Ainsley tried to push Rory out of her mind. She had been shocked to see him at the White House that morning. It was as if he saw her the second her news segment started and raced to where she was. If she was honest with herself she hoped to find him camped out on her doorstep when she got home, but he didn't know where she lived now.

For the last twenty-four hours while she moved her things into her new brownstone, she waffled from crying to anger. She'd spent all morning with cucumbers on her eyes to make sure they weren't swollen for her first day in her new job. Meanwhile, images of Rory in her bed played over like a sappy old movie.

A knock at the door interrupted her tree pose, and she gave up on a workout.

Shock for the second time that day coursed through her as she opened the door. Outside, there were rose petals scattered all over the doorstep, candles lined each step, and at the bottom stood Rory with more light pink roses. There was music playing from somewhere in the private stoop area covered by branches of an old Magnolia tree.

"Another peace offering?" she asked, standing at the top step. She was too scared to hope this was more.

"No, this is a love offering and an apology for being an idiot. This is me groveling for you to give me a second chance."

Her body shivered with excitement as he slowly made his way up the steps until he stopped to stand just one step below her.

"Did you say love?" she asked, hesitant to believe he could be mirroring the same emotions she had been struggling with.

"Yes, I know it's too early and a little alarming, but there is no other reasonable explanation for why you dominate my thoughts. I've been miserable thinking you would live so far away and worrying that some perfect guy with a trust fund was going to snatch you up. This morning, I accepted a new position at the training center. I'll have weekends off and thought we could at least try long-distance, but then I saw you on TV."

"You were going to ask me to do a long-distance relationship?" she asked.

"I was going to beg you to," he said, taking her trembling hand in his.

"But you said you're not capable of a serious relationship. You said you didn't have the capacity."

"I was wrong. You snuck into my heart, and I don't want to find out what it's like to be without you. I love you, Ainsley, and I would appreciate it if you would let me try to prove to you that I'm capable of being as serious as you need me to be."

Closing the space between them, she wrapped her arms around his neck and pressed her forehead against his.

"Okay, Sergeant. You have a deal."

He didn't wait for her to say anything else. Instead, he kissed her with adoration and desperation. They didn't come up for air until he picked her up and walked inside the brownstone, kicking the door closed behind them.

"Where is your bedroom?"

She laughed as he started up the stairs.

Epilogue

A INSLEY RETIED HER nighty for the fifth time, and her fingers struggled with the silky, delicate ribbon. It had been exactly one year since the first time Rory brought her out to his lake cabin, and she wanted everything to be perfect for tonight.

"Babe, where are you?" Rory called out.

Looking at herself in the mirror one last time, she walked out of the guest room into the living room at Rory's lake house cabin.

The moment he caught sight of her in the black lace, his eyes narrowed and he moved closer, but she stopped him with her outstretched palm.

"Not so fast," she said. Her plan was to distract him with this lingerie, but it was working too well.

"You greet me in this sexy number only to torture me?" Rory said, reaching for her and running his warm hands along her arms.

"Yes," she confessed.

"Minx." He smiled.

"I have an early birthday present to give you," she said, pulling the envelope from the silky robe she had over her shoulders and handing it to him.

His eyes scanned her body up and down before he focused on the envelope.

"My birthday isn't for another month."

"I know."

"Okay, but after I open this, will you let me get in my birthday suit and make love to you?"

A rush of heat flowed over her body, and she pressed her thighs together.

"Absolutely," she promised.

He opened the envelope and pulled out the tickets.

"First class tickets to Ireland?"

"To explore your Irish roots." She worried he wouldn't want to go on such a big trip, but the grin on his face proved she worried for nothing.

"First class. Baby, you shouldn't have."

"Only the best for you."

Rory's hands enveloped her before he sank to his knees. She hadn't anticipated that move which meant he would find his other gift sooner than she planned.

"I'm going to have to show you extra appreciation for spoiling me." His mouth was hot on her skin through the silk-and-lace top of her nighty.

Her head lolled back as she ran her fingers through his thick waves, and his hands began to explore her body. He lifted one of her legs to straddle his shoulder, and his mouth drifted over her stomach to her waist. He pushed her nighty up higher as he placed kisses on her thigh.

"Baby, you are the only gift I need," he said between kisses.

"Oh, then I guess I can return the other thing I got you,"

she said, refocusing on his face as he stopped to look up at her.

"Well, if it's more lingerie, I think you should just keep it." His sly smile melted her every time.

"Are you aware of how sexy you are, or does it just come so naturally you're oblivious?" she asked.

He kissed her hip bone with the most gentle touch while staring into her eyes, causing her to gasp.

"You were saying something about another gift?"

He reached up to untie the bow between her breasts, and his hand caught the metal weighing down one of the strands that she tucked inside the nightgown.

"I think I'm supposed to be the one kneeling for this, but you look so good at it." She moved her leg down off his shoulder and kneeled in front of him.

"Marry me? I love you, and I'm already yours forever," she said.

Rory's eyes widened as he held the thick white gold band she'd selected for him. She kissed his hand and took the ring from him before sliding it onto his left ring finger. It fit perfectly.

She looked into his shocked gaze which seemed to be filled with so much emotion she found her own eyes watering.

"You're asking me to marry you?" he asked.

"Yes. What do you say?"

"I say absolutely yes, on one condition." His hands wove on either side of her face before he kissed her deeply.

"I will accept any condition as long as you promise to kiss me like that for the rest of our lives."

Standing, he pulled her to follow him toward the fireplace. Reaching up, he pulled out a small blue velvet box hiding behind a picture frame on the mantle. She gasped, knowing what it must be as he sunk down on one knee.

"Ainsley Nash, I will marry you if you will marry me." He opened the box and presented her with a sparkling emerald surrounded by diamonds.

She knelt in front of him and kissed him again. "Yes," she whispered against his mouth.

Rory slipped the ring onto her finger, and they both laughed with relief.

"I love you, Rory Maguire. You're the only man who could one-up the perfect marriage proposal."

"I love you too, baby. Forever."

The End

Don't miss the next book in the Legacy of the Maguires series, *Strictly Off Limits*!

Join Tule Publishing's newsletter for more great reads and weekly deals!

If you enjoyed *Battle of Hearts*,
you'll love the next book in the...

Legacy of the Maguires series

Book 1: *Last First Kiss*

Book 2: *Battle of Hearts*

Book 3: *Strictly Off Limits*
Coming in June 2023

Available now at your favorite online retailer!

About the Author

Author of your next binge-worthy romance series, Stella has been plotting sexy, tear-jerker stories since she was old enough to hold a pencil. Born a Georgia peach, Stella loves all things country but calls the beach home even though she's currently living outside D.C. with her family. Most days she can be found drinking too much coffee, collecting lipstick she forgets to wear, and baking.

Thank you for reading

Battle of Hearts

If you enjoyed this book, you can find more from all our great authors at TulePublishing.com, or from your favorite online retailer.

TULE
PUBLISHING